For Jennifer, who continues to be the driving voice that I hear just when it is needed most. And for Serenity, who remains my loudest cheerleader and my biggest fan.

ASHLANDS
MIND OF THE MENCIST

BENJAMIN QUINTERO

This is a work of fiction. All of the characters, organizations, and events portrayed in this novel are either products of the author's imagination or are used fictitiously.

Ashlands: Mind of the Mencist

Published by Benjamin Quintero

http://www.benquintero.com

ISBN-10: 0985013400
ISBN-13: 978-0-9850134-0-0

Printed in the United States of America

10   9   8   7   6   5   4   3   2   1

ASHLANDS
MIND OF THE MENCIST

Chapter 01

Standing at the window of her classroom, a young girl was perched against the glass. Her long dark hair was straight and narrow, enough to rest easily on her shoulders. She wore a simple gray jumpsuit, a standard-issue uniform for the academy. The gray suit, laced with dark decorative bands of cloth, was enough to contrast against her subtle olive skin.

She could almost feel the heat radiating through the thin rigid pane of glass, but it was only her imagination. The thin pane of glass was merely a motion image that was cool to the touch, another small step for human evolution. The image distorted then rippled lightly where she had placed her hand. The young girl didn't care much that it was only an illusion or that the glass was only a holographic display to make every room feel like it had a view of the world outside. She didn't even care that it was a ghostly projection of an Earth that she never knew, an Earth with snow capped mountains and changing seasons. It would be one of here last moments to experience the hologram after all. Soon she would depart and start her life over again as she had done so many times before. This time was different however. She wasn't just moving across a state borderline or an ocean; she was going to leave Earth all together.

"...amara," a faint voice could be heard. Slowly, it came into the foreground, "Amara, I need for you to please take your seat." A teacher was standing next to a podium near the front of the class and had a concerned look on her face.

Amara turned to see the entire class filled with peers who were still seated and staring at her. She could hear a collection of low mumbling voices but struggled not to pay much attention to them.

"...what is wrong with her?"

"...just got up in the middle of class... ...losing it."

Amara paused for a moment, searching for her desk. It was the same desk that she had sat in all year and somehow it all felt so completely new. "I am sorry Mrs. McKinney..." Her throat was dry and the words had to be forced out. She licked her lips and cleared her throat but it did not help much. Finding her desk again, Amara sank into her chair. The thought of leaving Earth was unnerving, a new feeling for her.

Mrs. McKinney took her place behind the podium again and opened a folder that she had in her hand. A projection appeared to hover over the folder. It was a holographic display that all teachers used at the time for illustration. She swiped her hand across the image and a projection of Earth appeared. A vertical swipe bisected the planet, showing its various layers. Another swipe and it began to rotate slowly. Before she continued with her lecture she peered over to Amara one last time, "If you are not feeling well you are welcome to see the nurse at this time. Honestly Amara, this is not like you. If are you are okay then I expect you to behave according to the academy regulations."

Earth was a changed place and had been for countless centuries. Competing nations instituted a new level of accelerated learning. From birth to the age of twenty, students were enrolled into accelerated specialist programs. All public and private educational curriculums became tracks that predetermined the fate of each born child. From birth Amara was destined to be a Mencist, a military consultant of high intelligence and unwavering logical reasoning.

It was imperative that each Mencist have the logical reasoning of a human being with the apathy of a computer since they were often put in situations that required difficult military decisions to be made, decisions that likely resulted in mass casualties. Mencist undergo nearly two decades of intense psychological training and reprogramming. Despite genetic isolation during conception, all subjects were still unique in some way. Being human at birth, it was imperative that all Mencist share a unified voice to avoid favoritism of competing opinions. To eliminate any genetic variance the first 7 years of reprogramming were tailored to each subject. This can range from displays of violence and torture to physical abuse of the subject or isolation from human contact.

Despite several tragic historical events and countless protests the program was never abolished. Over the course of many generations, the Mencist program was perfected and a new breed of the human race was cultivated. Mencist academies were then regarded as the highest in honors. They bred Earth-born children who were raised to a level of intelligence that was thought to be otherwise impossible. A Mencist was still human but they all shared only the barest of emotions; confidence, anger, but mostly indifference and apathy. Logic and reason was their only compass.

Amara excelled as a Mencist amongst her classmates but something was happening. Perhaps it was the unknown of her future that made her uneasy. Not knowing was a position where she rarely found herself and it was difficult for her to grasp onto the idea that there was a future she could not extrapolate.

"Yes Mrs. McKinney I am fine," Amara replied shamefully. She could feel her mind coming into focused once again. Amara dwelled on the words, *academy regulations*. It sparked a bit of a chill down her spine to recall some of her early reprogramming. She continued to focus on her composure and it wasn't long before she began to feel like herself again.

By the time Amara was focused on the day's lesson a new projection was being displayed. McKinney had zoomed into the global until a single person on a city street could be seen. She gestured with a tapping motion onto the figure and the projection displayed the person in the well known anatomical position. "Can anyone tell me the closest relative to the human DNA?" McKinney asked in an assuming manner.

"The chimpanzee," a student in the back answered.

"That is correct," McKinney paused for a moment but Amara analyzed that it was only for dramatic effect. She gestured a pinching motion on the hologram to reveal a chimpanzee that was just outside of the projection. "I want all of you to ponder something for a moment. We know from the genetic research of our forefathers that the chimpanzees have a difference in DNA of about one percent. I want you to think about the intellectual gap that separates us from them. I want you to think about how far we've come in human evolution, how humans can compose symphonies and paint great works of art. Consider how chimps have barely managed to develop even the most basic of human communication skills."

McKinney paused and again Amara spent more time analyzing her mentor than she did consider her question. After all, Amara had already calculated the potential paths that her mentor was planning to take this lesson. The topic was meant less to teach them anything new and had more to do with reinforcing an idea, a principle shared by Mencists.

"Okay," McKinney spoke as if to interject their thoughts, "Knowing that we are so similar to a creature that we have still failed to effectively communicate with, I'd like for you to imagine what kind of being might exist out there if they were just one percent different from us? Imagine just one percent in the same evolutionary trajectory that we are to chimpanzees."

"You are talking about the Sigil," another voice in the class spoke out.

"There are many inexplicable artifacts out there that possess unknown alloys and technological advancements, not just the holy Sigil that you are referring to. Some would argue that these artifacts and their fabricated alloys are evidence of an alien species. What do you think, Amara?" McKinney turned to Amara, who was ready and waiting to respond.

"If I were religious I think that this would shake my belief. History has shown exactly that. Christianity was nearly toppled with the first discovery that we may not be alone. Belief in an Omniscient Rector, an all knowing alien as the source of human creation, became the popular opinion; more popular than the 20th century belief in a supernatural power," Amara didn't smile but she knew that her answer was not what McKinney was searching for. It was her way of being right without actually answering the question. She took some pleasure in toying with her mentors, and today was no exception for a battle of wits.

"I've never seen this holy Sigil, whatever it may be, so it is difficult for me to accept as tangible evidence," another student replied. Amara immediately recognized the voice as Emilia.

Amara turned to look at her rival classmate. Emilia was not especially tall but she had a very athletic build. Her short dark hair barely grazed the fair skin of her neck as she sat stiff in her desk.

Emilia continued, "In all of human existence we have not seen another living creature that shared our intelligence. Though we have discovered living creatures beyond our galaxy, most of them shared a closer resemblance to the primates that live on Earth."

"Do you think that we are special, Emilia?" asked McKinney.

"If science is right, we are a statistical probability. At this time it would be difficult to say but evidence would suggest that there could be an intelligent species beyond our own. Statistically speaking the universe is infinite and humans are constructed from a small finite number of elements." Emilia spoke in a voice that was monotone in nature. It was as if she was reciting from her databanks a textbook reply. McKinney's smile showed her satisfaction with that response.

"Okay class, that will be all for today," McKinney said. "I want all of you to have an answer to that question for next class." As she closed her folder at the podium the projection disappeared. "Amara, please stay after class, I need to speak with you."

Amara waited at her desk for the classroom to clear before she walked to the front. "You wanted to see me?" She asked in a polite tone.

Amara's polite tone was clearly an imitated form of friendly expression, one that they were taught to mimic when speaking with non-Mencist. It helped officers and civilians to feel more connected to someone who would otherwise appear as a living computer devoid of emotion. Politeness was more of a tactical response for a Mencist than a genuine reaction or kind gesture.

"Today is your last day. I am told that you will be moving to Serec. You will need these documents to approve your early graduation." Handing the documents to Amara, McKinney smiled saying, "You were one of my brightest pupils, even if you were also one of my most difficult."

Amara interpreted her statement to be an attempt at humor and struggled to crack an awkward but polite smile, another part of her formal training. She promptly reached for the documents and placed them inside of her carryall next to her tablet computer. "Is there anything else?" she asked. Amara stood motionless, while waiting for orders.

McKinney frowned a bit before speaking. "No... No that will be all. Good luck," she said.

Amara nodded. She determined that her mentor must have felt some kind of attachment to her. Perhaps her mentor was expressing some form of grief but it wasn't something that concerned Amara any longer than it had to. This would likely be the last time that she would see Mrs. McKinney and heartfelt goodbyes were never part of her reprogramming.

Chapter 02

Amara stood just inside the main doors that lead out of her building. Her final lecture was behind her. Gripping the handle of the brushed metal door that separated her from the outside, Amara turned back one last time. She studied the storage units that lined the walls of the academy, and listened to the ambient drone of the empty halls.

The door only required a light nudge for the motors to do the rest. As the doors slowly crept open Amara felt the dry gust of air push its way into the halls like the release of a compression chamber. Unfazed by the sudden rise in temperature she steadied the shoulder strap of her carryall before stepping outside. The natural light was slightly blinding at first but she quickly adjusted. The holographic windows inside may have produced realistic imagery but they hardly compared to the real thing. Even the low levels of ultraviolet radiation that they emitted to reduce vitamin deficiencies was barely enough to replicate the sensation of the Sun.

Amara felt more alive in the day light; perhaps it was a reaction to her early reprogramming, her isolation treatments. Still, she was very much aware that the sun was toxic now and had been for centuries. With an overabundance of trioxygen in the lower atmosphere and noxious gases from the last world war failing to disperse, the surface of the Earth left much to be desired. Outside of the holographic images, she knew nothing of the world that once existed. She felt it was better that way, not knowing exactly what was lost and not losing a fight to protect a planet that was destined for self-destruction. Amara pondered that if this world created humankind it also created its own destroyer.

Amara placed a small, inconspicuous device that pinched against her septum. The ring shaped device activated and appeared to create a small bubble over her mouth and nostrils. The bubble was almost entirely invisible with the exception of a few digital distortions that appeared whenever some pollutant came in contact with it. The device served two purposes; filter mild pollutants and a visual indicator that triggered if potentially fatal toxins were detected.

She walked down the winding pavement that lead through the academy courtyards and out into the streets. She wondered why the academy had courtyards, given that it was unsafe to be outside for more than a few hours at a time. With the building being as old as it was, she assumed that there may have been a use for them long before her time.

There was no rush to get home. Her father, a high ranking military officer, spent little time at home. She decided to stop by one of her favorite stores before making her way to their living quarters. Just down the street from her school, a small shop sold a number of random things. She liked the idea of a store that lacked any specialization and offered a little of everything. Standing just outside, Amara could read the sign that said *Happy Tree*. It was an odd name but it seemed fitting for being one of the only shops in that district that still sold live plants.

Walking through the open door Amara could hear the crackling of pollutants that had fallen into her hair and clothes. They were effortlessly vaporized by the thin barrier that screened the front entrance. Once again, the barrier distorted with each nano-toxin that was caught in its web. Inside, the store was mildly chaotic in design. Trinkets dangled from rotating stands and odd children's toys were piled carelessly into small crates. In the back, a glass counter encased various small flowering plants.

"Can I help... oh Amara it is good to see you again," an elder woman kindly greeted her. The elder woman appeared from behind a curtain of beads that led to a back room. Amara could see through the swinging beads that the room held the excess inventory.

The woman's face was weathered and worn but her smile was a sharp contrast, warm and youthful. The woman walked with a cane but it was never apparent to Amara why. She walked perfectly fine without the cane and yet almost never took a step without holding it in her hand.

"It is good to see you, Caryssa. I came by for one last trip through your lovely shop." Amara was being overly kind, perhaps a bit dramatic, but it seemed logically appropriate at the time. She decided to pull her kindness back and paused to remember her teachings. *If you are undeservedly kind, many will see it as an act of deception.* In a slightly less warming tone she said, "I need something for my travels. I may never return to Earth and would like a small keepsake of some kind".

The elder woman frowned. She was clearly upset to see Amara leave. Caryssa stepped behind the glass counter that held exotic plants inside. Grazing her hand across the glass, she motioned to the many groomed flowers. "Perhaps you would enjoy a fine plant. I can't imagine that there are many flowers like the ones you find here on Earth?"

"No, I don't imagine that a plant would survive the long trip. I am told that we will be in cryostasis for a very long time," Amara said as she shook her head. She continued to patrol the long glass counter and eventually

came upon rows of shelves. Each shelf contained glass
jars that were sealed with large cork stoppers. The
labeled jars varied in size and had small grains in them.
"This is new," she said as she pointed at the jars inside
the glass counter.

"Oh yes, that may be perfect for you. I just recently
received a shipment of seeds," the elder woman exclaimed.
She shuffled over to the counter where Amara was
standing. "They are not instantly beautiful like the plants
over there but, with some love and attention, you can
grow a fine garden. Best of all, you don't have to care for
them until you plant them. Seeds will travel quite nicely I
would imagine."

"I will take one gram of that one," Amara said. She
pointed to a large jar that had a blend of many seeds. The
jar did not appear very popular to Amara since it
appeared to still have a fresh seal. The card that rested in
front of the jar described the blend as 'A collection of
wildflowers and strains of grass.' Caryssa frowned.
Judging from the price, Amara's selection was clearly a
poor quality seed that likely held more unwelcome weeds
than it did hold prize winning garden plants.

"That will be two credits." Caryssa gently poured the
seeds onto a sheet of paper that rested on a scale. She
continued to add more seeds pinch by pinch until it was
exactly what Amara had requested. Caryssa then creased
the paper and poured the seeds into a small glass
container that was roughly the size of a locket. She
pressed a cork tightly into the opening and tied a thin
leather strap around the neck of the bottle. "It is not very
elegant but if you intend to keep it as a keepsake I
thought I would make it into a piece of jewelry for you to
wear." She handed the makeshift necklace to Amara who
kindly nodded as if to thank her for the gesture.

Caryssa held out a tablet that displayed the bill.
Amara noticed that there was no additional charge for the

necklace or the small container. It was likely a parting gift from the elder woman. Amara waved her wrist across the tablet and the transaction was complete. "Thank you for everything," Amara said in a genuine voice. The elder woman simply smiled and nodded as Amara turned and walked back into the street.

Chapter 03

Just outside of her apartment building, Amara looked up and could only see four maybe five stories before the haze began to swallow the building and everything around it. Visibility was fading as it often did in the late afternoon. The smog seemed fall from the skies and settle in the streets and alleys, and the pollutant disintegrator positioned on her septum gave off a familiar pinging sound. It was a warning that she had spent far too much time exposed to unfiltered environments. She had been outside for nearly two hours by now and it was about to reach dangerous levels of exposure so she hurried inside.

As she walked through the motorized glass doors and into the foyer that marked the entrance of her building, Amara could feel the cool filtered air that awaited her inside. She waited for the doors to close and the room to scan over her, killing off any contaminants. Finally the main interior doors opened and she stepped into the lobby.

To her right was a small desk where the security personnel were available to register and screen any guests. To her left were two elevator doors, each elevator displaying a range of floors that it reached. She did not bother to greet the security guard, she never did. Instead, Amara stepped into the second elevator on her left, the elevator that reached the upper levels of the building.

In a single motion Amara pressed the button for the 12th floor and then pressed her thumb against the identification sensor. It was the top floor in this relatively small apartment building and required identification to reach the private suites. As if to confirm her disgust over the arcane technology, she frowned and shook her head lightly. Amara was annoyed that the building had not updated to the more common wireless biometrics systems that analyzed passengers by their radio frequency identification implants, known as ID or RFID to some. But the building was something of a historical landmark, and there were lingering regulations that prohibited wireless biometrics within historical sites.

Her theory concluded that politicians were likely skeptical of what information could be ciphered by hackers through biometrics systems. Since most branches of the remaining governments were still in historical buildings it didn't take much to enact the law. Holding onto crumbling old buildings from a time before the biotech revolution was a tradition that she failed to understand. The frustration only lingered in her thoughts long enough to be irritating, but it quickly escaped her once the elevator doors began to slide open. She was home.

"Oh good you are home," a voice greeted Amara, who was surprised to find anyone home. The voice could be heard from the kitchen; it was her father. Before she could respond, the phone rang. Her father was quick to answer, "Miles here... Yes... That is correct, 0800 tomorrow morning... Thank you sir I will do my best." Miles hung the phone before poking his head out of the kitchen. "I thought we might have a classic meal before we leave, something fitting of Earth."

Amara snorted quietly to herself, "That is a funny thing to say. Earth is not exactly doing well, so what would you define as fitting?"

"It was hard to find but the beef was raised naturally, cloned but not synthesized. I watched him grind it myself. You may not even recognize the flavor." He disregarded her comment, as she had expected. Miles seemed almost in good spirits but she could not determine if he was excited over the quality food or if it was something else.

"What is the special occasion, Lieutenant Colonel?" Amara often called her father by his rank or by first name. It was another impersonal touch that came from her years of Mencist reprogramming at the academy. He was always proud of his position with the UMI and it became something of a running joke for him, but more of a routine or protocol for her.

"That is Colonel Miles Binson to you lady," he said with a smile. Miles quickly turned his attention back to a deep pot of steam. Sizzling sounds erupted from the kitchen as he stirred the pot and a splash of clouded water fell onto the heating elements.

She was always amazed at what kind of father he was in spite of what kind of soldier he had to be. He was ruthless in battle and gained considerable praise for his accomplishments and the reputation of zero tolerance for all militarized operations. She always knew that he wouldn't hesitate to strike down an opponent but it was perplexing that he could appear so warm hearted to her. *Reprogramming?* She thought to herself. Perhaps it was just the love of a father, yet another thing that she admitted to never understanding. Though they never talked about his past, Amara could only assume that he had his own form of reprogramming. She reasoned that it allowed him to carelessly balance his mental state between a trained killer and a loving father.

Amara knew that the promotion was inevitable. It was common to promote the UMI's most devoted and place them along the outer reaches of their iron grip. It was safest to have their most dedicated soldiers on the outer reach and focus their supervision on the places closest to home, Earth. To her misfortune her father was just that man, a committed ranked official of the United Military Initiative. She did not bother to force a trained smile since he wasn't looking. He would have known, better than anyone, that it was a fake display in spite of her best efforts. Instead, she made her way to her bedroom to pack her clothes for the move.

"...Remember, you only have to pack a light bag for the trip. The rest of our belongings will be packed and sent to our new house." Amara could faintly hear his words traveling out of the noisy kitchen and through the hall that lead into her bedroom.

She looked around her room, a neatly groomed museum that was organized into sets of right-angles. The matching nightstands stood equidistant from the bed post, and the table lamps were positioned uniformly on each nightstand. With sheets stretched tightly over the mattress, the bed looked the same as she had left it that morning. The pillows were organized at the head, and the bed covers were tucked just underneath the lip of the pillows. Under the pillows, the covers were folded over just once, no more, no less. The otherwise pristine room had bare white walls that looked to be painted over poorly. Faint shades of color could be seen underneath the thin layer of paint that now coated the walls.

Amara placed her carryall on the floor then reached underneath the bed and pulled out a small suitcase. Resting the small suitcase on the bed, she opened it and started to pack her travel apparel. Remembering what her father had told her, she only packed a few street clothes; some jumpsuits and a formal singlesuit. To her knowledge, there was always at least one formal dinner on the passenger vessels. She continued to pack other bare essentials, constantly reminding herself to pack light. The last item that she managed to squeeze into the suitcase was her keepsake, the small glass locket filled with her last memory of Earth.

Walking back out to the main living area, she could see her father setting the table. He was an unusually tall man; broad shouldered but slender at the waist. His dark hair was laced with shades of gray and it was cut in the standard military fashion, high and tight. His face had definite signs of a hard life as a soldier, a survivor of the many insurgent wars against the UMI. A few subtle wrinkles helped to mask a handful of what appeared to be shrapnel wounds across his chiseled faced. Though he never did tell her how he got his battle scars, Amara would not dare ask him of any of his missions; past or present. It was understood that war was something not to be discussed in their home, not ever.

"Please, have a seat," he said. Miles had already served the dish that was still steaming on its plate.

Amara quickly sat down to inspect the meal that her father was so proud of. At first glance, it didn't appear to be all too special. It was a bowl of pasta, served with a Bolognese sauce. He had placed some hand-sliced pieces of bread on the side that appeared to be coated in some form of oil and garlic. Amara twirled a run of pasta onto her fork and took a bite. She was pleasantly surprised, something was clearly different.

"Like I said, the meat is not synthesized. Even the pasta is real wheat, not a substitute." Miles smiled at Amara's curious look. She was clearly trying to analyze the flavors more than enjoy them. He took a bite and let out a quiet but savory sigh. "You cannot find produce like this anymore, not without paying unrealistic tariffs."

Amara was definitely shocked by his statement, or rather, what his statement implied. For such a strong military advocate, it would have been cause for reprimand to imply that globalization under the UMI was not an absolute solution to the worlds' disorder. She disregarded his comment as a momentary lapse in judgment. It was too uncharacteristic of him to feel so strongly against the teachings of the UMI or to imply that he knew of a better way to maintain the world's problems.

It didn't take long for his cheerful tone to turn back to his usual serious nature. Through most of their meal they sat quietly. There was the occasional moment that they would both look up, and Miles would awkwardly smile before they looked back down into their food. It wasn't until Miles had nearly emptied his bowl that he spoke.

"I want you to be strong. The next few years will not be easy and I know that you will be leaving your friends behind..." Miles was talking, if only to break the silence.

"...I don't have friends," she quickly interrupted.

Amara did not mean to sound spiteful, it was only the truth. She had memories of classmates and fellow Mencist but it would have been difficult to call them friends. Mencist were analytical thinkers, generally internal people and often misunderstood. Amara was no exception to this reality, and as a result, she rarely acknowledged her classmates as more than intellectual rivals.

Miles frowned but did not hesitate to continue, "We are going to Serec. My role there will be to show good faith that the UMI is there to support them. We will be investing in this settlement and their efforts, investing in their businesses, and growing the population there. It will be a real honor for me."

And an opportunity for another promotion, Amara thought to herself.

"The UMI is being very kind to an otherwise ghost settlement. If you had not told me about Serec or the town of Harvest, I would have assumed that it was just another star in the sky." Her tone was firm. Amara was letting her father know that she was not dumb enough to believe that this entire operation was out of charity.

Miles smiled proudly at how quickly she saw through his guise.

"The UMI has shown interest in Harvest. Even if I knew, I couldn't tell you why," he explained. It was clear that Miles had the answers but Amara wasn't going to crack him so easily. She simply nodded her head and gave her eyes a subtle roll to avoid the dead end conversation.

"0800 tomorrow you said? I overheard you talking to someone on the phone." Amara was merely changing the topic. It was clear that she was not going to get much information from her father.

Words of kindness from Miles would have fallen on deaf ears. Amara was impartial to staying on Earth but it was the life that she had known since her birth. She did not know if her hesitation to leave Earth was a side effect of the institutionalized world of a Mencist or if it was her innate human nature. There were some things that even reprogramming could not eliminate, and human fears of the unknown ran deep.

"...sharp," Miles promptly replied, "You should get to bed early. We have a full day tomorrow."

Amara quietly finished her meal then helped by cleaning the table and moving everything to its proper place. She took special care to align the centerpiece before turning toward her room. Tomorrow would be a full day, a day like no other. It would mark the first time in her life that she was not waking up to dress in her uniform and attend the academy, like she had done her entire life.

A full day indeed, she thought.

Chapter 04

Amara slept well but the morning still seemed to come too quickly. It wasn't long before she was out of bed and groomed for the day. Her usual breakfast was waiting on the table; it was a calorie bar, a substitute meal that contained all of the synthesized proteins and nutrients required for a balanced breakfast. The taste was fairly bland but it did have a hint of sweetness and a nutty texture that was meant to simulate some form of grain, perhaps oatmeal or granola.

Miles was nowhere to be found but Amara suspected as much. He was likely at the docking station, barking orders at the staff. It was in his blood to ensure that a fleet ran smoothly, even if it was not his own. Quickly grabbing her carryall and her suitcase, Amara headed to the main door.

Standing at the door, she grazed over her old living quarters one last time. Amara felt like she was leaving something behind but could not think of anything. Her luggage had all of the bare essentials and her remaining personal items would be shipped to her new home. So why was she feeling so empty handed? After a long pause, Amara stepped out and left any remaining worries at the door.

It did not take long for Amara to reach the loading station. Once there, she could see piles of cargo being hauled onto a massive passenger vessel. She was already too close to read the ships name since the hull's smooth sides beveled upward too quickly and the name was well out of sight. Amara did not need to read the ships name however, there were signs everywhere. Each cluster of signs guided passengers down the right while the fleet personnel and cargo were being carried to the left, toward the rear of the ship.

It was not too uncommon for space ships of this size to dock in her city but it was a bit exaggerated in size. Amara was not expecting a particularly large group of travelers to be roaming to the outer reach and yet this ship could serve ten thousand passengers in comfort. She studied the signs one last time and followed their directions to the passenger registration booths.

Behind her, Amara could see mobs of people waiting in a reserved area. The area was surrounded by a beltway that separated the crowd into organized lines. She could hear the intercom from time to time but their words did not seem to comfort the ever-growing crowd of people.

"Please be patient. We are boarding everyone in the order that they have been registered." The voice on the intercom was tired and shared a hint of frustration. "Stay behind the line or we will invalidate your boarding pass!" The voice called out in a raised tone and the crowd slowly shuffled behind the line on the floor.

"...we've been here for four hours!"

"...this is ridiculous... ...what about her?" Amara focused on the irate voice that shot out from the crowd. She turned to see a small group of individuals peering at her with accusing eyes.

Amara pulled out her boarding pass, a thin flex-glass sheet. The sheet was just smaller than the palm of her hand but was filled with a stream of digital information. She waved the boarding pass over the ID in her wrist before handing it to the attendant.

"Not to worry Miss," the flight attendant stopped to read her boarding pass, "Miss Binson. We have an unusually large group of passengers today, many of them Class C. The vessel is broken into three chambers and each chamber is designated by their Class. You have a Class A executive boarding pass, so I can assure you that *those* people will not be disturbing your time with us."

The flight attendant only briefly glanced over to the crowd. She frowned and shook her head before she slid the pass over a scanner. Offering a polite smile, the attendant returned the pass to Amara and gestured for her to enter the boarding tunnel. "Welcome aboard."

Amara nodded then collected her things before she turned one last time to see the crowd. Most of them appeared to be factory workers and miners. Many of the people looked to have their families with them as well but Amara focused on a woman who was holding her child. The woman had long blonde hair that fell ragged onto her fair skin. Her eyes were focused on her child who must have been no older than three months, still covered in wraps and torn bed sheets. The woman caught Amara gazing in her direction but did not react. They briefly locked eyes before the woman looked back down at her baby and began to rock and sooth the child over the noise of the crowd. With her curiosity satisfied, Amara then stepped into the boarding tunnel and made her way onto the massive ship.

"Amara!" Miles was waiting at the end of the boarding hall. He raised his hand but his tall stature needed little help to stand out.

Dressed in his formal military uniform, Miles seemed to stand even taller as he displayed a classic suit that was sheltered in metals and accolades. Amara found it amusing that, for all their technological advancements, the UMI still insisted on physical medals. Perhaps not everyone found the same value in digital goods as she did, even then.

Picking up her pace slightly to greet him, Amara waved to acknowledge his attempts. "You left without me." Her tone was matter-of-fact. Though she was not upset with him, she was curious enough to probe for answers.

"I wanted to make sure that everything ran smooth. I needed to know the name of the person who was responsible for moving our personal items onto the cargo ship." His response was just as Amara wagered; her father was trying to run the ship. "There should be another cargo arriving soon and the movers should be arriving at our quarters as we speak."

"This ship is massive. I hope I don't get lost." Amara was serious. Once on the ship, there was a distinct lack of signs like she had seen on the loading station.

Miles grabbed her boarding pass then activated it by sliding his wrist ID across a small digital strip at the bottom and speaking, "Miles Binson". The pass displayed an interactive directory. "There, I've registered my ID into your directory so you should be able to find me if we get separated. The pass is already registered in your name so you should have full access to the directory. Once you activate it, the pass will act as a full navigator through the ship though I doubt you will need it. After the formal dinner, we will be heading to our quarters for a long nap," he said with a smile.

Amara knew that he was trying to be sarcastic. His *long nap* would be a twelve year period in cryostasis. Though it wasn't necessary for a period of twelve years to use cryostasis, it was more cost effective to let the passengers sleep. It meant that the ship could board thousands of passengers and not need an excess of clean running water, food synthesizers, and other space consuming supplies.

"What about Class C passengers?" Amara was genuinely curious. Cryostasis was not inexpensive; it was only less expensive than catering to a class of citizens who were accustomed to only the finest of living conditions.

A flight attendant overheard Amara's question and quickly answered it. "There is no cryostasis for Class C passengers. Class B passengers are mostly the crew members who cycle their shifts. There are also a few middle class passengers who can afford a partial sleep program for these types of long journeys." She turned to Miles before continuing to speak, ensuring that everyone in the conversation was included. "Each crew member has one active year of service for each journey, so two years for a round trip."

The flight attendant had been standing near the opening of the boarding tunnel, next to where Amara and Miles had been standing. It would have been easy to miss her if Amara had simply entered the ship and continued to walk.

Amara pondered for a moment. If that mother and her child were boarding this ship, there was a strong possibility that the mother could die or the child could grow up without twelve years of education. It did not seem right. She continued to inquire more, "Does this mean that the children will grow without education or that the elderly may die in this journey?"

The flight attendant frowned. "There are an unfortunate few deaths among the Class C passengers for flights like these. Anything can happen, just as it does here on Earth. We must supply them with synthetic nutrient supplements and fluids, as well as law enforcement and accredited education. Childhood education is completely automated through our computerized learning system. Arguably, they will receive a higher level of education in our custody than they would on Earth," the flight attendant spoke proudly. Though her responses were a bit robotic and rehearsed, it was clear that she had a genuine confidence in their program.

"...higher education?" Amara interrupted.

"Yes. Many of the Class C passengers are industrial and public service employees. Normally they cannot afford the fine education that you have received. Our educational program has received accolades from prominent UMI officials." The flight attendant noticed the intense look on Amara's face so she continued to explain, "Many Class C passengers are only here because their employers have paid their way. Work on Earth is growing scarce and increasingly expensive, and companies are moving their efforts elsewhere. For many of them, this was the only choice."

Amara was somewhat relieved that they followed the same Earthan regulations of education and human rights. It could have been easy for them to neglect Class C but it seemed that the UMI had done some good for extending rights beyond Earth's atmosphere. She was beginning to see why her father was so faithful to the cause. Perhaps there were *some* good intentions to grow out of a unified military society.

After taking a long pause to absorb the information, Amara nodded. She had more questions but did not want to interrogate the attendant. She lowered her head slightly to show appreciation for the brief lesson and the attendant returned the gesture to show respect for her attentiveness. Amara looked up at her father and kindly gestured with her eyes that she was ready to leave.

Placing his hand on Amara's back, Miles guided her down the hall. Together they navigated through the lavish corridors with their boarding pass in hand. The corridors were dressed in velour drapes that strung along the walls and she could sense that the floors were padded with thin memory foam. Amara concluded that the decorations served for more than pleasant appearance.

The aesthetics were clearly there to appease the high society but they were deliberately chaotic. The many folds in the velour drapes increased the angles in every hall and the padded floors muffled her every step. Amara ran her fingers along the wall as they walked; even the texture of the paint had micro-abrasions to increase the angles. It was all intended to mask the hollow drones that often plagued space vessels. She could not hear a single sound beyond the mumbling chatter of other passengers; no moving machinery, or hollow clatters, nothing. If she had not just walked onto this ship herself, it would have been difficult to know that this corridor was not on solid earth.

"Your room is here and I will be just down the hall. I will meet you in the main ballroom for dinner. You should wear your best outfit," Miles said with a grin. He was already dressed in his uniform so it would not surprise her if he was planning to investigate the ship further.

Stepping into her room, Amara could see it was a bland space compared to the halls outside. The room contained only a small desk and chair with a large cryogenic bed that filled the center space. The bed looked like a sealed tube and was semi-cold to the touch. Some effort was made to dress up the bed with a skirted sheet to cover many of the pipes and wires underneath. It was a feeble attempt, Amara thought.

Placing her items carefully on the small writers' desk that was built into the wall, she promptly changed into her formal singlesuit. The glass locket was not particularly exotic but it was the only resemblance of jewelry that she remembered to pack; it would have to do.

A small bathroom was connected to her room so Amara decided to inspect her hair. She never was very good at dressing up and her father's only sense of fashion was how short he could cut his own hair. Instead of spending a long time playing with her hair, Amara twisted it into a spiked bun and ran a long decorative pin though it. The pin was easily four maybe six inches in length and it looked surprisingly elegant for such little effort; once again, it would have to do.

Just outside of her door, the noise level was increasing. The heavy foot traffic told her that the festivities were likely to begin soon. Amara quickly grabbed her pass and rushed out the door to follow the crowd. The slowly shuffling crowd eventually made their way through the corridors and into the main ballroom that seemed to open up significantly from the other rooms that she had seen.

The room was enormous and littered with crowded tables. Amara promptly guided through a short menu of options on her pass and eventually selected *Dinner Seating*. The pass became translucent and Amara held it up like a digital periscope. The augmented visuals displayed a digital marker of her exact seat and an optimal path through the winding tables. Once she identified her seat, Amara lowered the pass and set out to greet her father, who was already seated.

Miles was having a playful conversation with a woman to his left. She was an attractive woman, wearing a red dress over a layer of sheer black. The dress seemed to slide up her leg on one side and resembled a twenty-first century fashion but it also fit the general theme of the ballroom's decor. The woman's attention seemed unwavering as she chatted with Miles, laughing at his jokes and playfully caressing his leg on occasion. Amara recognized her tactics as a classic mating ritual and judged her to have a seventy percent chance of success.

To the right of Miles was an open seat that was reserved for Amara. Next to Amara's seat was an older man who she recognized as a political figure, but his exact position in government escaped her. She could only remember that he was somewhat of a failure and pariah in the political circle, yet maintained a considerable wealth from his time in office. The rounded table was filled with other high powered officials, though some of the men and women were clearly there as escorts.

Once everyone was seated, it was an opportunity for Amara to observe the fellow passengers on the ship. The room felt more like a masquerade party than a formal dinner. Some guests had entire tables reserved only for them and their promiscuous entourage.

As the night went on, there was less dining and more drinking. The once elegant appearance of many participants devolved into an over sexualized display. The lights faded along the walls of the massive ballroom and many groups moved their personal parties to the confines of the darkness, although it was not hard to see what they were doing and the music was not nearly loud enough to hide the moaning voices that rocked back and forth.

Amara frowned. It was a disgusting display for her but one that she would have to grow accustom to if she planned to maintain the status that her father had built for the family name. As much as she disapproved, this was the life of high society and it was not going to change for her. She looked up at her father who was clearly not at ease with exposing his daughter to this environment.

"I am sorry Amara. If you have finished your dinner, you are welcome to head back to your room. I did not expect things to get to this so quickly." Miles was almost sheepish. It was an expression that he rarely demonstrated beyond the confines of their home, but she understood his distress.

Shaking her head, Amara put his thoughts to rest, "A Mencist is hardly ever a person to worry after." And she was right. Her reprogramming meant that she had to grow up quickly or suffer through a life of unspeakable reprimands. Though she did not agree with the disgraceful public displays, it was not something that would leave lasting impressions on her.

Miles only gave an uncomfortable grin in response before the woman to his left grazed her hand along his forearm. "It looks like your daughter is not the little girl you thought," the woman said in a seductive voice. She was clearly trying to initiate and Amara concluded that she might succeed before the night was over, her chances were improving.

Miles had been drinking much heavier than she had ever seen but it appeared to be customary for these elaborate dinners. After a quiet sigh, his focus turned back to the woman and they continued to speak.

"Is it common to overindulge on a long journey?" Amara threw the question out to the table. Her only intent in asking was to avoid a conversation centering on her, especially in such an awkward and sexualized situation.

"Life is short. Even with all of our vast technology we have limits when it comes to extending life..." The elder man to her right barely slurred the words out.

"...auto- rejuvenative human tissue," Amara interrupted. She did not mean to sound so exact in a conversation amongst inebriated participants but it was her only nature.

"Exactly," the elder man exclaimed. "Look at me. Thanks to modern medicine, I may have the sexual potency of a boy in his prime but my body will continue to age like it would have a thousand years ago."

The elder man had reached under the table and slid his hand onto her leg while he was speaking. "We can only stop time in cryostasis but that is hardly the way to enjoy life. That is not living." As he spoke, his hand continued to crawl up, nearly reaching her inner groin.

"So you indulge yourself in one night to make up for the years you will spend in suspended animation?" Amara was asking, but in a rhetoric tone.

Amara could almost see the reasoning in their twisted logic. There was one critical flaw in their motive however. Since time stood still for them, they were not losing any time in their own lives. It was only an excuse to take their pleasures to the extreme, yet another reason to indulge in carnal pleasures.

Sensing the boney hand that was now groping at her, Amara barely flinched but gently lifted his hand. With a polite trained smile, she positioned her thumb and index finger over one of the many pressure points and effortlessly dislocated one of his knuckles. Not intending to apply enough pressure for a clean break, she may have fractured his frail bone.

The extent of the elder man's injuries was difficult for Amara to assess since he drew his hand back quickly and yelped, clutching it in agony. The man's painful scream lured Miles' attention but he was too late to see the action unfold. It all happened so quickly that Miles was left clueless.

"It appears that our friend has injured his hand." Amara had spoken with an arrogant but annoyed tone. Her overtly polite attitude did not go unnoticed by Miles however.

"Then we should have him escorted to the sick bay. They may have questions," Miles replied. His tone was accusing as he glared at the elderly man. But still, it was difficult for Miles to mask his smile when his attention returned to Amara.

Perhaps Miles' view of a delicate young lady was being clouded by a father's affection. He was beginning to understand exactly how dangerous his daughter really was, how dangerous a Mencist could be. He knew better than anyone that a lifetime of militarized education has certainly had its advantages and his daughter was no exception to that.

"This would be a good time for me head back to my room. I wish all of you a safe journey and I hope to see you again," Amara spoke in a clear and proper manner. She politely bowed her head before speaking again. "Perhaps next time it will be in a more civilized setting." Amara was entirely serious though her comments did raise a chuckle from the table.

"Oh Amara," Miles stopped her. He gave her a sealed plastic package that contained a myriad of pills. "We'll need to take our sleep pack before we forget."

Amara remembered fragments of conversations about the sleep pack. It was a small pill pack that was meant to ease the symptoms of cryogenic sleep. She was admittedly nervous about taking the mysterious collection of pills and their strange color and texture only amplified her suspicions. Amara had never been placed into cryogenic sleep but she felt her confidence rise after witnessing her father carelessly toss the pills into his mouth and swallow them with a tall glass of water. She quickly did the same.

As she walked away from the table, Amara turned to see the woman in red continuing to caress Miles and whisper in his ear. To Amara, the woman looked desperate for attention; a sensation that she had never experienced herself. Outside of Amara's lightly pursed lips and a subtle lift of her eyebrow, her curiosity about the woman did little to change the expression on her face. Leaving her thoughts of the promiscuous woman in the ballroom, Amara turned again and headed down the main corridor that lead to her sleeping quarters.

Arriving at her room, Amara was greeted by a flight attendant waiting just outside her door. The attendant was holding a cryosuit; another measure for easing the effects of cryogenic stasis. Though the suit was not required, it increased the success rate of reanimation significantly. Amara took the suit and headed into her room. Closing the door behind her, she quickly undressed and stepped into the suit. Once inside the suit, she allowed the attendant into the room to assist her with the procedure.

The attendant helped Amara climb into the bed and gently closed the lid. Pressing a series of buttons, the attendant was operating the dials like a veteran; mechanically calibrating the system looked like a mindless effort for her. In moments she had activated the sleep chamber. Offering one last smile, the attendant faded the lights and left the room.

It was silent inside of the sleep chamber. The little space that she had to move did not seem like enough at times. It was barely enough for her to clutch the locket that still hung around her neck. The wait was beginning to put her on edge and it was not much longer before her mind started to wonder.

Amara thought, *how long does it take for this device to...*

Chapter 05

...to work. As if her very thoughts were suspended in time, Amara awoke to the sound of her bed decompressing. It was unclear how long she had been sleeping and the 24 hour clock on the wall was of little use. Her disorientation told her that she was no longer on Earth.

Though it was barely noticeable, Amara could sense a slight difference in the gravitational force. Her body felt slightly heavier and her weight seemed to press down on her chest a little harder than before. The shift in gravity was only easy to notice because of the sudden change in atmosphere from Earth to her current location. Of course it was only sudden for her because time had stood still until now. Feeling the weight press harder on her chest, Amara found it hard to breathe for a moment. She stopped to calm her nerves from the suddenness of it all, and her breathe slowed and stabilized with each inhale followed by a controlled exhale.

With her breathing stabilized, Amara could hear the sounds of shuffling luggage and crowds of people stomping past her room. The clamor of bumping shoulders and banging cargo that the people made in the halls sounded much more urgent than it should have been, and Amara only rolled her eyes subtly to confirm her disgust. She thought back to the Class C passengers who were waiting to board on Earth and saw no difference in them from the selfish hustle of the so-called Class A passengers.

Logically, if the noisy crowd were to form orderly lines and wait patiently, the process could have been at a minimum of twenty-two percent faster. At least that was her best estimate at the time. She did not bother to analyze their boarding procedures too deeply upon her arrival to the ship, though Amara still found pleasure in calculating the faults of others.

A faint voice over the ships intercom suggested that passengers prepare their personal items, and Amara listened again to the chatter that waited just outside of her door. The clamoring passengers, the intercom announcements, the weighted feeling on her chest; all of the cues must have meant only one thing; she had arrived at Serec.

Seconds after her discovery that she had landed, Amara was uncontrollably disoriented. Her head spun violently and her vision was doubled over. She immediately staggered to the bathroom and barely reached the sink before vomiting a thick blue fluid that had the consistency of motor oil. Amara could sense that the bile was unsurprisingly cold as she wildly convulsed and it continued to flow in small spurts.

Amara let the hot water run while she hovered over the sink for moment, trying to catch her breath. It was all she could do to keep the drain from clogging. Rinsing out the last of the cold blue fluid from her mouth, Amara wiped the steam that clouded the mirror in front of her. Using a nearby hand towel to dry her face, she looked into the mirror that had already begun to cloud again and waited for the nausea to pass over. She had seen better days than today, and the fatigue from her long sleep had left her in worse condition than she had expected.

It took some time to readjust but she eventually changed out of the cyrosuit and into suitable clothing, one of the jumpsuits that she had packed in her suitcase. Once she had collected her things, Amara held the glass locket tightly in her fist. It was still cold from having taken the journey with her in bed. She left the room without looking back and was glad to never have to do that again, at least for a long while. Judging by what Miles had told her, it seemed that Serec would be their new home for years to come.

It wasn't long before Amara found herself heading toward the door from where she originally boarded. She followed the flow of the crowd who seemed to be doing the same, finding their way to the main boarding doors. Several minutes had passed and she had not yet seen her father. Remembering that he was just down the hall from her, Amara suspected that he could not have been far. Amara stopped for a moment and raised her boarding pass, then navigated through the options once more and selected *Locate/Miles Binson* who had already been registered earlier. Holding the pass up to her eye, Amara scanned. The augmented overlay displayed a beacon in the crowd, a target not far from her current location on the ship. After charting a mental note, Amara put her pass away and followed the instructed path.

In minutes Amara met up with her father who was standing near the main doorway but partially out of view and leaning against a wall. He was a bit more serious than she had seen him in recent days. Perhaps his vacation was over and his work was just beginning.

While scanning the crowd, Miles noticed Amara and he raised his arm to catch her attention. Amara did the same to let him know that he had been found. She made quick work of navigating the crowd with her small suitcase, but still found it annoying that people were scattered in such disorderly patterns. She tried not to focus on the little things but something about basic human nature always seemed to get under her skin.

Privileged to have received Mencist reprogramming, Amara was doomed to live a life where people around her could never understand what she now considered common sense. Most people would consider her manner of thought to be a series of computer algorithms more than a natural selection of cerebral impulses. Her definition of common sense was on a different level than most. Being a Mencist was both her privilege and her curse.

"Did you sleep well?" Miles asked in a humorous tone. Amara's tired eyes and flush colored lips were a sure sign of her morning experience. She was not amused by his comment.

Miles managed to crack a smile but it faded as quickly as it came while his eyes remained fixated on the crowd. She knew that large disorderly crowds always placed him a little on edge. It was likely the reason why he was also partially hidden with his back against the wall.

"I wish you would have warned me that the waking sickness was so terrible..."

"I didn't want to worry you. Besides, it is a good experience for any future soldier. Most of our enlisted are forced to undergo sleep cycles as part of their training. Many noncommissioned officer ranks, like Mencist, do not often get the opportunity." Miles was attempting to make light of an otherwise grueling experience. Amara could see through his feeble attempt but she still appreciated the effort.

Miles knew Amara well; she would have likely bombarded him with questions before the sleep cycle, questions that were best answered through experience. Bothered by the fact that her father knew her so well, she snorted quietly to herself. Despite the sickness that still swirled in her gut, the experience was worth noting.

Amara took a second to create a mental log of the experience. Like a cerebral stenographer, she recorded every minute detail of how she felt before and after the chill. She then dictated the almost indiscernible lapse in time to herself in order to commit the feeling to memory. Like folders in a filing cabinet, Amara had many memories tucked away.

Cataloging of information was just one of the many skills that a Mencists was trained for. The theory behind information cataloging was that knowledge helped to make better choices, and knowing the past would imply smarter decisions for the future. With each cataloged memory Amara, and many Mencist like her, lose a bit of themselves. Personal memories, the ones that define their individuality are cast aside to make room in the limited space of the human brain, an unfortunate side effect of her gift. Even still, scientists argue whether the memories are truly lost or if the network of connected thoughts has simply been broken in the cataloging process.

As the doors begin to open, Amara immediately noticed many changes. The most obvious difference was that no one was using pollutant barriers. She pondered if Harvest had been enclosed in a biosphere or some other advanced methods to purify the local oxygen supply, but her questions would have to wait. The crowds began to clutter impatiently around the doors and Amara took a step back and pressed against the wall to avoid from being sucked into the wake. She briefly glanced up to her father who was shaking his head in disgust and she imagined that he must have at least shared some of her feelings about the crowd's selfish behavior.

"And these are the people who are supposed to be preserving our human decency, the high society..." Miles continued to shake his head slightly as he spoke, pursing his lips as he observed the crowds' sporadic movements.

"It can't be helped," Amara replied, "After all 'human decency' is an oxymoron." Her voice was monotone and each word was iterated without remorse.

Standing motionless with her father, Amara watched the crowd rush through the doors that were barely ready to greet them. As much as she disapproved, it was almost entertaining for her, like watching a herd of wild animals fleeing a predator on the open planes. Unsurprisingly, she thought of most people to be beneath her, and looking out to the flock of talking heads only served to validate her feelings.

Miles took his attention away from the crowd that billowed out of the doorway. His attention was absorbed by the words that his daughter had spoken, and he could only stand there and watch her obsessively counting the bodies that rushed by. Holding a stone faced look, Amara's eyes seemed to be the only thing that shifted from side to side with an occasional twitch of her lips. Not a moment went by that Amara wasn't fully committed to her lifestyle as a Mencist and she was good at her work. He questioned if he had given her a successful life at the cost of a happy life, or if her view of 'human decency' meant that she did not consider herself to be human. Why would she; a Mencist was simply more than a human, it was the next evolutionary step for mankind.

"Are all of these people moving to Harvest? It seems like an easy way to overpopulate a small settlement," Amara's voice was enough to break the trance that Miles was under.

"No... No," Miles replied. He was still a bit lost in his own thoughts. "Harvest was the first settlement and the only colony with an extraterrestrial export. That means this is the only space port on the planet right now. Most of the Class A passengers will head to some of the larger cities. Radha for example has become quite the metropolis and is focused prominently on global trade within Serec."

"Serec seems to function much like Earth did in the early twentieth century." From her cataloged history lessons, it was Amara's closest reference to what Miles had described. Earth had not been under UMI control until the thirty-fourth century, several generations before her time.

"You could say that, but don't be fooled. This is not Earth." His comment sounded more like a military order than a suggestion. Amara took his words to heart and nodded to acknowledge his warning.

With those final words from Miles, he grabbed his travel bag and gestured to the doors leading outside. The doorway had thinned out and only a patient few people were left waiting for their turn to exit, it was a reminder for Amara that not everyone in this world had selfish intensions.

Standing at the gangway of the massive space ship, Amara combed the pier with her eyes. The disapproving look on her face was quickly washed away by a stern gaze from her father. As if to apologize without words, she returned a trained smile and held his hand briefly. It was becoming very clear that her actions would reflect on him and the UMI. She would need to be more careful, at least when she was around her father.

Standing on the side deck, Amara waited patiently for the gangplank to be cleared of other passengers and cargo. She had spent all of her time along the interior of the ship, not noticing that large oval windows dotted the exterior hull. The outer deck that she stood on appeared to be accessible and Amara was certain that the view must have been breathtaking. She regretted her decision to go directly to her sleep chamber after dinner since it would have been a sight to catalog, though it was difficult to say if one could see anything at all while traveling at near light speeds. Harvest may have been the only space port but they lacked even the most primitive equipment required to load passengers. Peering down at the makeshift gangplank, it was immediately clear to her that

Harvest received more cargo than it did receive travelers from Earth.

Dragging her luggage in one hand, Amara's other hand was clenched with anxiety over the unknown. They had arrived to their new home; a settlers' planet, for what seemed to be light years from her place of origin. As Amara reached the end of the gangplank, she felt her first step of solid earth. The ground was thankfully paved though potted and rough, and the paving appeared to exist only to prevent heavy machinery from sinking into the silky white sands that she could see in the distance. Amara was beginning to understand what her father meant when he said this was not Earth; she had never seen a desert so deprived of color.

"Amara is that you?" a young man's voice could be heard over the shuffle of busy feet and the mumbling sounds of a crowed space port.

The young man was rushing toward the two from the gates that separated the space port from the town just beyond. He clumsily stumbled for a moment as he attempted to wave and attract their attention. The young man was wearing an occupational coverall that was earthy in color. The ragged clothes fit loosely on his dusty frame and oil-stained cheeks. When he had finally reached them, Amara could see that he was a few inches taller than her, even though his shoulders were a little slumped and his head was lowered. Panting like a dog it seemed, he struggled to catch his breath but eventually did. It appeared that he had been running to catch them, an already poor impression for someone as judgmental as Amara.

"Are you here to show us to the house?" Miles remained as serious as ever but Amara could sense that he was making an effort to behave more like a civilian and less like a career UMI representative.

"Yes Sir, Colonel. My name is Emrys... Emrys Hughend," the young man replied and his voice crackled when he spoke. Amara could see that he was unreasonably nervous but she did not feel that it was appropriate to raise attention to it, not yet.

"You must be the son of Cole Hughend," Miles quickly prompted with a smile on his face. "Your father is doing great things here, I can feel it. If I don't see him today please let him know that the UMI is here to help."

"I will... Colonel... The mines haven't paid yet but we are hopeful." Emrys addressed Miles properly but did not return the smile.

The gritted muscles along Emrys' dirty cheeks and the lightly clenched hands were signs that only a Mencist would notice. Amara could sense that there was something more to their brief exchange. Again, she bit her tongue and decided against prodding for answers. She was making a valiant effort to be on her best behavior, at least for one day.

They quickly collected their bags and began to follow Emrys out of the port and into the small town of Harvest. The buildings throughout the town were striking; they shared a closer resemblance to art than architecture and their curves seemed to follow the shape of the horizon. As impressive as it was, the town appeared small, microcosmic by comparison to her home on Earth. It did not take long before they made their way to the town center by foot, a handful of city blocks it seemed.

"The buildings are quite impressive," Miles observed.

"Their beauty is partly a side effect of their function. We do get violent sand storms at times and the simple curved design helps the sands blow past us more easily. The entire town is structured such that, as the winds increase so does the opposing pressure." Emrys spoke proudly of the achievements in Harvest, though he could not claim to have designed the architecture that protected the town. "This allows us to slowly grow this settlement into a metropolis of our own someday without the need for external devices like biosphere barriers or nanomist radiant shields."

"This colony..."

"...settlement," Emrys promptly interrupted Miles, "We prefer to call our home here on Harvest a settlement."

The long silence was enough to tell Amara that Miles was taken off guard. He was not accustomed to being interrupted, and especially by a younger man, a civilian at that. Emrys crossed many lines without knowing it, but Miles appeared to be in good spirits that day. Or perhaps he was only playing the part to keep in good graces with the people of Harvest.

Still, Amara understood what Emrys was implying. Colony was the name often used to describe an inhabited territory that was typically associated with a parental chain of the UMI. By correcting Miles, Emrys meant to draw the line in the sand and let him know that Harvest was an independent town just like every other territory on Serec. Being so far from Earth meant that Serec was out of reach from the grasp of the UMI, and calling Harvest a settlement implied a certain kind of liberation from UMI control. Though she did not care much either way, Amara pitied the young man for holding onto an ideal that was sure to crumble under the weight of the UMI; not today, but someday. She had seen it before, with planets closer to Earth than Serec. Amara understood as well as anyone that the UMI's control was absolute.

"This... settlement... appears to have grown," Miles stated. His mischievous grin was a clear response to Emrys' interruption. He paused to witness a small family walking into a restaurant. The restaurant was weathered on the outside, but through the windows he could see that it was well kept inside. "The military briefings had not

implied that there was a strong enough economy to
support this kind of living."

"We manage but there are classes of citizens here;
some do better than others. The economy on Serec is a
fledging form of capitalism." Though prompt and
respectful, Emrys' responses were barebones and lacked
any emotion.

For Amara, it was not clear if Emrys simply found
politics and economy to be boring, or if he felt that the
UMI was not welcome on Serec. She wondered how many
others felt like him, felt like the UMI did not belong.

"You addressed me by my first name. Should I know
you?" Amara spoke in her usual apathetic tone.

"It has been a long time. We went to the same
academy for many years and even shared some classes
together." Emrys jumped to respond with a smile on his
face. "I understand if you may not remember me. We
were very young when my parents took me out of the
academy to come here. I eventually finished my training
here and went to work for my father soon after."

"You do not strike me as a Mencist." Amara was quick
to observe his very human and somewhat awkward
demeanor.

Emrys stuttered for moment, not quite sure what to
say. "Oh... Oh I am not, I am an Engineer. I received
standard enlisted education here. It was all that they
offered at the time. Only in the last five years has there
been a Mencist academy," Emrys explained. He could
sense that Amara's comment was referring to his behavior
or lack of Mencist composure but only replied, "Besides,
you would be surprised at how quickly the mind heals."

Looking up, Emrys saw a puzzled expression on Miles'
face but quickly gestured to keep moving. Miles had a
stare that seemed to imply that something in Emrys' story
did not add up. "We really should keep moving," Emrys
pressed as he nervously rushed the guests down the street.

Amara stiffened her shoulders. She was mildly insulted by his last statement. Had he implied that she was damaged for being a Mencist? Again, reminding herself to be kind and gracious, she did not want to press the issue in the presence of her father. Amara was certain that she would have another chance to test this supposed childhood friend.

"Here we are." Emrys pointed to a house that stood alone, the only one of its kind in Harvest.

The house had a direct view of the town center and stood slightly elevated over most of the other buildings. It was quite impressive and easily many times larger than her small living quarters on Earth. Speculating on the perks to come in the future, Amara was beginning to appreciate the benefits of living in Harvest. If she knew how, she might have smiled.

"I believe the house has been pre-furnished by now. Our cargo should have been received several weeks ago though I suspect that we may have some unpacking to do," Miles stated in a pensive tone and had already started inspecting the house as he spoke.

"But when we left, our things had not even been packed. How did they arrive before us?" Amara was questioning the lapse in time. Had the journey taken longer than expected?

At first, Miles looked surprised that she did not know the answer. "I see," he said, realizing that it was fairly emergent technology that was not cleared for the academy yet. "Though we have passenger ships that are capable of near light speed travel, there are still limits that require us to remain within controlled parameters. Non-organic cargo is capable of traveling at jump speeds, and the UMI is willing to afford the potential loss of product but not the loss of a human life. The technology is still unproven."

As if to say goodbye to Emrys, Miles nodded and grabbed his things. Before they could step into the house, Emrys blurted out a few words to catch their attention one last time.

"Colonel, I was wondering if Amara would be busy tomorrow," Emrys' voice began to crack again. "You see, I have the day off and would gladly show her around town."

Rubbing his chin gently, Miles paused for a moment to think. "Yes," he said. "I think it would be good for her to rekindle an old friendship and learn about her new home." Miles sounded genuine but Amara could tell that he was still playing the politician, earning the trust of this Cole person that he mentioned earlier. She was not amused to be loaned to this stranger as a show of good faith, but she complied anyways.

"Ok fine," Amara spouted in a begrudging tone. "I will see you tomorrow." She did, after all, have more questions of her own. With those final words, they watched Emrys nod politely and walk back toward the town center.

Chapter 06

Pushing the door in gently, Amara waited for it to
open on its own; it did not. She waved the ID in her wrist
across the handle but it did not respond. Finally, Amara
pushed harder against the door until it was wide enough
to walk through. She was curious that the door did not
respond to her biometrics, but she concluded that it
would be yet another change to grow accustom to. Emrys
had insisted that they meet there but she was beginning to
wonder why exactly.

Her eyes scanned across the small seating area that had
little more than a handful of tables. Noticing a man and a
woman sitting in the far corner, her attention became
focused on them for a moment. The dark-haired woman
had a long dress that was clearly meant to be formal but
Amara frowned. It looked almost ragged to her, even
though there was not a thread out of place. The woman
rested her hand on the table and her companion smoothly
reached and placed his hand over hers as they continued
to talk. Amara wondered if they were data-linking, but
why then would they still be communicating traditionally?
Their smiles irritated her but she had little time to dwell
on them since Emrys appeared through the door behind
her.

"Oh good, you are here," Emrys responded in a slightly
winded voice. He looked to have run quite a distance but
Amara appreciated that he took the time to dress in
something marginally better than what she saw yesterday.

His coverall was more fitting like a singlesuit but it suited his subtly muscular build.

"Do you run everywhere you go?" Amara spoke in her usual monotone as her eyes scanned down to Emrys who was huddled over with his hands on his knees.

Emrys only smiled at the slight inflection in her voice, something that only he noticed. He knew that Amara was genuinely curious but he opted not to reply. Instead, he gestured for the two to be seated and Amara promptly followed his lead. Pointing to a booth that rested against the large windows that dressed the front of the restaurant, Emrys waited for Amara to seat herself. He paused for a moment, as if to consider the thought of sitting next to her but quickly navigated to the booth seating across the table instead. Amara barely noticed his brief struggle and only stared blankly at him, waiting for Emrys to finally choose a place to sit.

It wasn't long before a waitress stepped up to their table. With a smile, she greeted them both and quickly took their orders. Amara watched as the waitress navigated a menu of options on her small digital pad before she walked away and then out of view.

"Interesting," Amara noted without explaining her thought.

Inspecting the plain metallic table, Amara was surprised to see such low tech equipment. No holographic displays, not even a digital screen could be found in the table. Peering underneath the table, she saw that it served little purpose but to hold their food and drinks. There were no wires or even an outlet to charge her tablet.

Somewhat regretful that she did not bring her tablet, Amara thought that it would have helped to pass the time. Her expectations for the day were low and a few video games would have eased the boredom that was sure to come.

"You are wondering why we don't use a self-serve ordering system." Emrys was making a statement but waited for clarification before he explained.

"...and why people don't use data-links for private conversations," she said as she motioned to the couple that were still holding hands over the table.

Emrys did not respond immediately. He only smiled but in a way that seemed to irritate her even more, he could see that much on her face. He decided to speak before his smiles would get him into any more trouble. "Anyone born here on Serec does not receive the UMI mandated biomedical augmentations. Those of us born on Earth have mostly disabled them or simply chosen not to use them since we are a fading population here."

"What about biometric RFID?" asked Amara.

"Still functional," he swiftly replied, "We try to keep the things that make sense. Data-link is somewhat dated but is so widely used throughout the ranks of UMI that it would be too costly to change." Emrys shifted back in his seat as he saw the waitress coming to their table with two steaming plates.

Carefully positioning the plates in front of each of them she only said, "Be careful, the plates are hot. Enjoy your breakfast." She quickly paced away to greet two gentlemen waiting at the front door.

Amara looked down to the meal that she had ordered, Eggs Benedict. She was pleasantly surprised at the presentation. Her first bite did not disappoint her expectations either. Accustomed to synthesized and substitute foods, it wasn't hard to impress her sense of taste but Amara could see that this small bistro took pride in their dishes.

"Did you sleep well?" Emrys asked. He stumbled with each word, as if the question may have been too personal to ask.

With a full bite still in her mouth, Amara politely shook her head. She covered her mouth with one hand but decided against speaking since the bite in her mouth was larger than she thought.

Emrys could see the tired look in her eyes. "It will take some getting used to. The days are about as long as you find on Earth but we have about two weeks less, some months are slightly shorter to compensate."

"Why is it so bright at night?" Amara asked curiously after swallowing.

Amara could only recall the diffuse sky that looked like an ever-present twilight. She loved the sun; even on Earth, the warmth was a tingling sensation on her skin. Even still she had her limits, and Amara was left craving a few solitude hours of darkness and restful sleep.

"It has to do with the tilt of Serec and the location of Harvest. You managed to arrive in our summer season. The days do grow quite long, I would recommend good shutters until you are accustomed to the seasons." Emrys was showing signs of confidence. It must have been encouraging for him to feel like he had something to teach.

The conversation about the bright night sky went on and Emrys continued to explain the unique qualities of Serec and Harvest. In his words, he sounded happy in Harvest, but it was difficult to read him and understand his true feelings. His glistened and distant eyes told a different story from the words that escaped his lips. Through all of his awkwardness, Emrys still had a guise about him that Amara could not break down. She was mildly intrigued to have found someone like him in this town.

Noticing two empty plates, the waitress quietly stepped up to the table and smiled before she said a word. "Is there anything else I can get for the two of you?"

"The check..." Amara spoke quickly, giving Emrys little chance to speak. Shocked that Amara was so quick to leave, Emrys was still happy that she did not want any more. After their meals and drinks, he feared that he may have miscalculated his budget.

With a friendly smile on her face, the waitress held out her small tablet. The tablet was mostly black but displayed a thin holographic image that was blue in color and rested nearly flat against the surface. Totaling thirty-five credits, the slightly raised images displayed their check and detailed the items that they had ordered.

Emrys breathed a sigh of relief. With a confident smile he raised his hand slightly to let the waitress know that he would be paying. Amara did not argue. He read the ticket one last time and Amara could practically see the gears turning in his head as he calculated an appropriate tip for the helpful waitress.

Swiping his wrist across the tablet, Emrys watched as it turned from its aqua blue color to a hard shade of red. The once warm and polite smile on the waitress was reduced to a scowl as she gazed at Emrys who tried two more times, but the results were the same.

"Just charge it to my father. He will understand." Amara spoke sharply.

"What's his name, Sweetie?" The waitress had a tone that was almost meant to humor Amara. Her frustration was obvious, and the raised brow and pursed lips did not help to soften her words.

"Miles Binson, I am his daughter," Amara said proudly. Her voice was slightly raised to make sure that she was heard the first time.

The waitress was suddenly smiling again, but it was a reluctant smile. Amara could see that the woman had no love for the UMI but was smart enough to understand their influence. With a forced smile, the waitress looked down to her tablet and cleared the credit warnings from her screen.

"If you tell your father how much you loved our food we can just forget about the check... Just this once; how does that sound?" The waitress asked and Amara only nodded at the proposal. It was enough to clear the bill.

Amara knew that her name would be enough to raise eyebrows. From the moment she landed on Harvest it was clear to her that she would have some influence on a small struggling settlement. Having a high ranking official like her father endorsing their restaurant would surely be beneficial to them, that much was obvious. It was an exploit that she could not use often or her father would certainly hear about it, but it felt like an appropriate time.

Despite being proud of herself for asserting her position, she was disappointed to have to use that tactic in a place like this. She looked across to Emrys who was bashfully counting his credits with a puzzled look on his face. Puzzled about her own strange feelings, Amara said nothing. She felt sorry for him but not the spiteful pity that she may have expressed for anyone else in this position. It was more like a genuine empathy, even if the emotion was quite faint.

Wanting to catalog this feeling and the shameful look on Emrys' face, Amara took a mental picture. Closing her eyes, Amara repeatedly constructed the image in her mind in order to commit it to memory. She was more intrigued by the emotion than the event itself, so she narrated the image to herself, committing a script that followed the image in her mind. As a Mencist, data and intelligence gathering was something of an expertise of hers. Though this event lacked any tactical relevance, it felt important enough to catalog. She did not yet know why.

Saying nothing and giving no notice, Amara casually stood to her feet and began walking to the front door.

Emrys, still lost in his counting, realized that he was alone at the table and nervously scurried out the door to catch her. Standing outside, Amara was already waiting for further instruction.

"You wanted to show me around," she said. Her arms were crossed which only exemplified her impatience for open or undirected situations like this. There was no plan, no directive, only time to meander through the small town. It was easy for Emrys to see that it was irksome for her.

Emrys only smiled in return. It seemed like his eyes would disappear into tiny slits whenever he smiled the way he did.

Finally fed up with his condescending grin, Amara blurted out, "Can I help you?"

"Did I do something wrong?" he asked. His smile melted into more a subtle smirk.

"You shouldn't mock me, Emrys. I am not in the mood, in fact I am never in the mood for your smug gestures," she exclaimed. Her hands were noticeably clenched onto her arms which were still crossed.

Emrys struggled to keep a steady face. He never meant to aggravate her, only the opposite. "I would never mock you. If you would like to know more about me and the things I do, perhaps a question or two would help," he spoke calmly. He did his best to appear at ease and unaggressive. Perhaps his cool perception would reflect on her, at least it was what he had hoped.

"I will ask when I am ready," she said. Without direction from Emrys, Amara chose a path and started walking. It would be some time before they spoke another word to each other.

As they trotted along the passages, Amara studied the buildings and their structure. What Emrys had implied yesterday was more accurate than what she had first imagined. There was more to the buildings than their aesthetic appeal, they were constructed from a kind of metal substance that she had never seen before.

She stepped up to one of the buildings and grazed her finger tips along the smooth metal. What appeared to be a rustic and weathered surface was actually an illusion, a result of the thin-film interference in the metal. The metal was almost cool to the touch and shared a matte luminance that only intensified at shallow angles to the sun.

Amara could not decipher the specific reasoning but her best guess was that the metals contained some form of nanotech to direct the sun away from the settlement. It would explain why it was nearly mid-day in their summer season and she could feel little more than a few beads of sweat on her forehead.

As she continued to walk further and further from the town center, the alleys quickly opened into broader pedestrian streets and the tall elaborate buildings were replaced by smaller but still elegantly designed huts. The outskirts of the settlement appeared more chaotic. Huts were positioned in a radial fashion that faced the town center but there were no visible paths beyond one, maybe two huts. Each ever-increasing ring of huts was not cleanly aligned to the ring inside or outside of it, and the paths followed more of a serpentine pattern than the long narrow paths of the inner circle from where she had come.

Upon further inspection, Amara could feel a breeze blowing through the serpentine paths. It suddenly became clearer as they approached the outer ring. Though the paths appeared to be chaotic, there was a method to the madness. The buildings and huts seemed to serve as a filter or guide for the heavy winds that blew just beyond the settlement. They dampened the heavy storms that seemed to rumble across the ocean of white sands and managed to keep the people inside safe.

Both Amara and Emrys sat down on a bench that overlooked the ocean of sand. Amara studied the clouds that seemed to move much more quickly than anything she had seen on Earth, telling her that there must have been strong wind currents that circled above them. She wondered if the currents stayed there or if they were being kept away by the deceptively protective buildings that surrounded them.

After some time was shared on the bench, Emrys finally spoke to break the long silence. "I used to come out here a lot when we first settled on Harvest. A lot has changed in the last ten years or so." His voice was once again distance.

As if he was reminiscing on the events that occurred in the last decade before her arrival, Emrys sunk back into silence next to Amara. On occasion, he would gesture for Amara to look away from the white sands. The blinding whiteness was beautiful but damaging to the eyes and he found himself reminding her of this often. They had been sitting on that bench for nearly a half-day. It was not exactly how he had expected to spend his time with her, but any time was a treat for him. He wanted to smile but dared not to in her presence.

"You said that we knew each other." Amara interrupted the silence with a bold question. It was as if she was repressing the urge to ask him, like she had been thinking about it since yesterday.

"I knew you. We went to the same academy. We only spoke once." Emrys was nearly at a mumble. He never looked at her; instead Emrys continued to focus on the sands that swirled in the dying breeze.

"We spoke once?" Amara was surprised that Emrys would be so friendly to someone that he had spoken to only in passing. A single conversation seemed like hardly enough to cultivate a friendship. "I must have made quite an impression," she said. Her tone was more informative than playful.

"You impressed me long before then," Emrys replied without thinking. He was still lost in the sands but quickly came to realize what he had said. "I... I mean to say that I have a pretty good memory. I was a Mencist in training after all."

Emrys bashfully scratched his head with his left hand. He intended to do so more to cover his blushing face than scratch any itch that he may have had. As he raised his hand and Amara could see a scar across his forearm, one that wrapped over his arm several times. It was a class of scar that she remembered vividly, the results of a disciplinary whip that was used in her early years of reprogramming.

It was unusual for anyone to have those scars on their arms. Typically discipline was administered on the chest or back, a place that would easily be covered by the standard-issue UMI uniform. Though it was considered necessary for the reprogramming procedure, permanent scaring was only meant to serve as a reminder to the subject, not a scarlet letter.

Something looked very familiar about the scar on Emrys but she did not dwell on it much. The thought of a disciplinary whip made her cringe and it was difficult to look beyond her own encounters. Flashing images of her past were enough to force Amara to push her thoughts onto another subject, one that did not remind her of the past.

"We should head back. It looks like the winds are going to pick up." Emry pointed to the clouds that started to form and grow dense. He motioned in the direction that they should take and Amara quickly followed him through the serpentine paths, back into the town center.

"Can I see you again tomorrow?" she asked.

It seemed like the day had passed so quickly and though it was still very bright outside, she could see that the sun had nearly fallen behind the tall buildings ahead of them. It was well past lunch and reaching into the dinner hours. Amara was amazed that the long days could seem so short. Her first full day on Serec was not eventful but Amara felt that it was exactly what she needed after a long journey through space, a day to reflect.

With a shining smile that didn't seem to fade, Emrys nodded and lightly said, "Anytime, Amara."

Those words seemed to ring in her ears, *Anytime, Amara.* It was not the words so much as it was the way he said it. She could not place it, but she was starting to feel like there was some truth to what he was saying. Perhaps they did know each other at one time. His words felt warm and touched her more than she would have imagined from a simple phrase. With her obsession of cataloging, it was difficult for Amara to say if he was simply a lost memory, a fragment of her past.

Emrys paused for a moment to think. It did not take long for him to decide where to take her, "Meet me at the same bench on the outer ring. There is something that I would like to show you."

Eventually finding their way back to the town center, Amara thanked him and walked away. She was a little baffled at why she had thanked him however. Having paid for brunch and practically giving herself a tour of the town, Emrys did little more than follow her around. She still thanked him and was genuinely happy to do it. There was something about him that she still had not figured out. Hoping that perhaps tomorrow would unveil more answers than questions, Amara wondered up the road and back into her new home.

Chapter 07

Several years earlier...

A young girl was standing in the courtyard of the academy; she had been there for some time. Her pollutant indicator warned that she had little more than 30 minutes remaining before toxin levels would overcome the barrier. She did not seem to care, at least her appearance said as much.

Gazing at a single flower that stood alone in the poisonous air, the girl had been motionless and unresponsive. She was caught in a trance of wonder. *How?* She posed the question to herself, wondering how something as delicate as a flower could survive. Caressing the velvet-textured petals of the flower, the young girl was amazed at how dainty they were. If she knew how, she might have smiled.

The prismatic array of colors on each petal made the flower appear almost metallic. The girl questioned if it was a random occurrence or an effort to adapt to the smog-filled air and encroaching iron structures that surrounded it. In any case, she found it to be beautiful. She could not help but be absorbed by the stark contrast of a flower that was struggling to survive in a world that would rather see it dead. Barely hearing the shallow sounds of a student who yelled from a distances, the girl remained fixated on her subject.

"You have to come inside!" the voice yelled, but the girl did not listen.

Another voice called out, a more familiar voice, "Amara! The instructors are coming! Please, you'll get us all in trouble."

Amara turned to see her classmate, Emilia. Emilia and the others were standing at the main doors and making wild gestures with their arms for Amara to come back inside. The worried look on their adolescent faces told Amara that trouble was just behind them, and they were right.

An instructor erupted from behind the crowd of students. One of the students tumbled painfully down the short flight of stairs that lead to the ground level of the courtyard. Even at the distance that Amara stood, she could still hear the young students' arm break clean from the sudden stop at the bottom. The screams would take longer to come, as Amara could see, the student was in shock. The cries that erupted soon after did not help to slow the instructors' pace. The instructor did not lose a single step as she stomped by the winching student on the ground and targeted for Amara.

As the instructor treaded heavily, Amara could see a small dark stick in her hand that was barely larger than her palm. With a single slashing motion, the instructor whipped the stick downward as she continued to walk. The small stick extended to be slightly larger, about the size of a swords' hilt. From the almost invisible distortion that seemed to flow from the tip, Amara instantly knew what it was. It was not the first time that she had seen a disciplinary whip.

"Students under the fifth grade are not allowed outside of the academy. You have been warned before, you knew that this was coming," the instructor said in reprimanding tone. She whipped the stick downward one more time and Amara could see the distortion slither around as it danced

in the air. Settling to the ground, the distorted line began
to sear a thin charred line that smoked and crackled with
tiny sparks of light.

Amara was overcome with fear and could barely stand,
let alone attempt to escape. Holding in the thumping in
her chest, Amara's legs felt like wet noodles and her body
would not respond. All she could do was watch as the
instructor cranked her arm back. With her heart racing
and her hands clenched, time seemed to stand still for
Amara. *Move... Move... Move!* She screamed out in her
own mind, trying to break her paralysis. After all her
efforts to react, she was only successful in closing her
eyes, raising hands over her head, and bracing for impact.

The loud crackling sound of the whip echoed through
the courtyard and Amara screamed. Her screams however
were out of fear of the sound and anticipation of the pain,
but there was no pain. She opened her eyes but they were
clouded from a mixture of tears and dust. Her heart raced
so fast that everything around her felt like a blur, like a
dream. A shadowy figure stood over her, separating her
from the instructor. It was a young boy who was dressed
in the academy uniform.

Once Amara was able to regain her composure her
focus returned as well. When she finally could assess
what had happened she realized that the struggle was still
taking place. To create some space between her and the
others, she crawled away on her back. Standing to her
feet, Amara saw the boy who had taken the blow instead
of her.

The tip of the whip was entangled around the boy's left
forearm and had already seared through the long sleeve of
his uniform. Amara watched as the two went back and
forth in a tug of war. Every time the instructor would
pull on the whip the boy would pull back with all his
might. Visibly irritated, the instructor finally pulled the
whip back in a sharp motion. It was easily enough to

sever the boys arm if she had not turned the whip off just seconds before retracting. The pull did not sever his arm but it was enough to toss the boy to the ground.

"You can thank him for taking your punishment," the instructor snorted. She took one last look at Amara and shook her head in disappointment before walking away.

Amara slowly walked up to the young boy who was now clutching his arm. He was obviously in pain but was trying to hide it. Still shocked from the events that unfolded so quickly, she saw him there and realized that it could have been her; it would have been her if he had not interfered.

"Why would you do something so stupid?" was all she could say.

Amara didn't mean to sound so accusing of someone who had just saved her from certain anguish but the words felt right. Perhaps her reprogramming was starting to take effect. Somehow she saw a logical reason for being punished but no reason for a stranger to risk his life to save just one other being. His math was irresponsible and reckless.

In return the boy merely smiled between brief wincing flashes of pain. He said nothing for some time but continued to smile in a fashion that only served to irritate her. Amara wondered if he was still in pain or simply mocking her because his smile felt out of place for such a grim situation. His arm was clearly cut deep but the searing heat kept the wounds from bleeding nearly as bad as they should have.

"Are you mocking me?" Amara asked.

"Never," replied the boy. It was the only word that he could muster as another wave of pain overcame him briefly.

"Well... I suppose a thank you is in order." Amara spoke with a sharp tongue and an unforgiving tone. She still questioned why the boy smiled so obsessively at her but could not help but thank him for his heroic yet thoughtless actions.

"Anytime, Amara." The boy was clearly in pain but seemed to put his mind at ease around her. "Is this what you were looking at?" He pointed to the lone flower that stood between them.

He hobbled over to the flower, bent down, and clipped the flower at the stem with his finger nails. Holding the flower by the stem he picked it up gently and extended it out to her.

"Here you go," he said in a polite tone. "Now you can take it inside with you."

Amara's eyes widened. She could feel the rage bubbling inside at the sight of her treasured flower being plucked from the earth. Words could not express what she was feeling and tears seemed like the only response that she could assemble. Before darting past him and back into the academy building, she cranked her hand back and slapped the flower out of his hand.

Unable to fight to pain any longer, the young boy collapsed. Dizzied and tired, he rested on the ground and listened to the nearing voices grow louder as they came to rescue him. Still wondering what he had done to deserve her angry response, the boy closed his heavy eyes and let the darkness take him.

Chapter 08

It was another sleepless night for Amara. The light from the diffuse morning sky began to bleed through every nook of the shutters that she had in her windows. Even with the shutters, Serec was proving to be a challenging place to adjust to. *Tonight I will try using a sleep shade,* she thought to herself. Perhaps a shade over her eyes would serve better than the shutters had promised to do for the windows.

Amara quickly ran through her usual morning routine. In the end, her bed was neatly made and her sheets were tightened to near military standards. She placed her decorative pillows as a finishing touch and made her way downstairs. Not wanting to be late, Amara grabbed an apple and made her way out the door.

Walking through the town and the serpentine paths, she bit into her small breakfast. What appeared to be a slightly discolored apple from Earth was in fact grown on Serec. Amara could instantly tell from her first bite and was surprised that they would grow and transport crops over the common approach to synthesizing. It had the same texture as an apple but the taste was unlike any that she had tasted. The flavor was much sweeter, almost too sweet for her taste, and it seemed to leave a gritty aftertaste in her mouth. She was not sure if it had to do with the unique mixture of nutrients in the soil or the methods that they used to grow cash crops on Serec.

Either way, like most things on Serec, it felt similar and yet very different from her home planet.

Amara eventually reached the bench that they had agreed upon and Emrys was already waiting. She first tried to sit down next to him but he quickly stood up and brushed a bit of white sand from his coverall. Noticing the collection of sand on his lap, she wondered how long he had been waiting for her.

"Were you waiting long?" she asked.

"Not long," he replied.

Amara knew that he was not telling the truth but did not want to press him. There was no point in knowing the exactness of his time, and Amara found that most people lied about such a question. It was typically a rhetorical question, much like asking someone about their day and expecting a positive response.

"There is actually something I wanted to show you, something special." Emrys wiped his hand out of fear that it may have been damp. He reached his hand out and offered to help Amara back up from her brief time on the bench. She accepted.

Letting his hand linger with hers, Emrys guided her away from the town and into the white sandy dunes. Eventually he gently let go of her hand. Though it felt right to be holding her hand, he knew that it meant much more to him than it did for her. Amara only curiously followed as they traversed the uneven terrain.

Emrys handed Amara a pair of sunglasses and insisted that she wear them. "You can experience similar symptoms to snow blindness out in the open dunes," he reminded her again. Emrys stopped and waited for her to put them on. He seemed especially concerned for her but Amara did not question his insisting that she be safe.

If it were not for the shimmering heat that distorted the horizon, the white sands of Serec looked more like snow capped mountains than a desert. Amara noticed something different from the deserts on Earth. There was a surprising abundance of greenery but they seemed to exist only as small islands, surrounded by the white ocean. On these islands, she could see a small sickly forest of mangroves and other ocean-side foliage.

"Aquifers," Emrys explained after witnessing the puzzled look on her face. "Most of the water on Serec is underground, oceans of water in fact. The aquifers are not as far reaching as the oceans on Earth but they run quite a bit deeper. Unfortunately many of the aquifers are salted."

"Salted? That explains the mangrove trees," Amara analyzed.

"Exactly, you may find a few fresh water islands of pine and other Earth-like evergreens but not in this area. We are standing over the Great Abyss, one of the deepest oceans on Serec." Emrys spoke confidently, like a navigator with a trusty compass in hand.

Amara was a bit unnerved at the thought of standing atop of the deepest oceans. Suddenly her footing felt less stable, but it was only her imagination or the weakening in her knees. Every step seemed to make a sound that creaked. Turning to look back, she had lost site of the town. Even the tallest structures had disappeared behind the steep dunes. They were stranded in the vastness of an ocean of white sands.

"Don't worry, you'd have to fall through a couple thousand feet of sand, rock, glass and stone to reach the waters," he said with a chuckle.

"Now you are mocking me!" she observed.

"Maybe just a little," he replied with a wink and smile. Amara's cheeks her blush as she knew that it was slightly deserved. His light tone helped her realize that he was only being playful.

Walking over one last dune, Amara could see what Emrys had in store for her. A small vessel was standing, barely erect, in the sand. The ground around it seemed to be frozen in time, the soil scorched by its trajectory, and the sands around it barely moved. It had an ominous nature that made her stomach uneasy.

Being there made Amara feel on edge. Still bothered by Emrys' attempts to mock her, she was growing ever more agitated. It was as if she had mistaken her anxiety for frustration. She knew that Emrys was taking her to some place 'special' but she was not expecting this kind of sensation.

When they finally reached the vessel, she could see that it was a sophisticated dropship or escape pod. It was much smaller than what she had anticipated, enough room for two young adults or one fully developed man. Through the glass panel, Amara could see that it was an exceptionally long hollow space. She found it strange that the space inside appeared to be fitted for a considerably large person, someone with above average height.

Amara watched as Emrys calmly slid his hand along the side of the pod. As he pressed down on a nearly invisible latch, the pod decompressed and opened. Emrys motioned for her to step inside, at which point she promptly refused.

"It is safe," he said as he crawled inside, "There is enough room for both of us. I can't turn on any dials until the door is locked down. You didn't come all this way just to walk back home did you?"

Amara looked at him with scolding eyes. His last comment sounded more like a dare than a vouch for confidence. The cool air that escaped from the pod was inviting and seemed to only lead to more questions about this mysterious pod. Pacing around for a moment, she eventually built up the courage to go inside. Amara stepped into the pod and laid down next to Emrys. She fidgeted around but eventually settled in and watched the door lock and seal.

Inside, Emrys reached across the cramped pod and bashfully pressed a toggle switch that rested next to her. As he reached, Emrys could feel her long hair fall onto his shoulders. A brief flow of her scent was enough to rattle his nerves and Emrys felt his heart drop into his stomach.

"Should you be touching that?" she asked in a disapproving voice. He only smiled, but slightly.

"It's okay I come here all the time. This place has some kind of religious significances or something, but you won't find as many believers out here, not like on Earth. Nobody really knows how it got here, but it was clearly made from some very advanced alloys." Emrys felt himself getting chatty, doing anything to calm his nerves. He tried his best to avoid any awkward silence in such close quarters.

"Explain exactly why I am supposed to care," she stated as if growing increasingly impatient. She motioned as if to cross her arms, if there was room to allow it; but to her dismay, there was not.

"You know; if the world ever came to an end I would wait for you right here." His voice was serious if slightly trembled. His nerves had clearly taken over but she did little to notice it or his chivalrous comments. Wincing in frustration over the words that came out of his mouth, Emrys knew enough to understand that death was not exactly a romantic topic of conversation.

"That is such a funny thing to say. You are a strange little boy..." she said.

"...Little boy, who is mocking who now? I am two months older than you. Besides, this is the safest place on the whole planet. At least that is what my Old Man told me. He thinks this pod was built by some alien race, long before we ever settled here..." Feeling increasingly gawky with each sentence, Emrys could not help himself as he rattled on about technology and their inner workings.

Amara's awareness faded. She was soon lost in thought but could still hear Emrys running on about the greatness of this device. There was something about his story that resonated with her, something that sounded familiar. It was not quite the same as any story or fact that she had learned about but more like bits and pieces of many historical truths.

"...it doesn't rust, it doesn't wear down, and even the life support and cryogenics are still functional." He would have gone on forever if she had not brushed her hand against his, even if only by accident. Still, it was enough to quiet him.

For a brief moment, in his silence, she appeared to let her guard down. Letting out a big sigh, Amara simply laid there and watched the day sky roll past the clear panel. The panel was a window to the world outside, something that she had barely noticed until now. They both gazed through the clear glass-like surface and watched the sky turn 3 shades of red. The sun was fading and the stars were beginning to glow a color that she had never seen back on Earth.

The reality of living on Serec was sinking in quickly. Amara relaxed her shoulders and tilted her head back into the seat. She asked, "Why are you being so nice to me?"

Given her brief knowledge of Emrys, her question was an honest one. After the life that she had lived, it was easy not to trust anyone. For Amara, trust was an intricate equation, one that required more parameters than what she knew about this young man. She could read his kindness but his reasons why were simply inconclusive.

"Isn't it obvious?" he replied in a nervous tone. His voice was still shaken but he coughed once or twice as if it would help.

Turning toward her and shifting his weight to one side, Emrys leaned in slightly but Amara did not move.

She was still none the wiser to his actions and stared puzzled over his now sweaty appearance. Just then, the air pressure released with a rumbling sound and the door opened.

"What are you doing in here? You little misfits are desecrating a symbol of our Omniscient Rector!" An older woman was waving her walking stick at them.

Both, Emrys and Amara, leaped out of the pod. Emrys leaned in one last time and Amara watched as he flipped the little chrome switch back to its original position. They both quickly stepped to a safe distance from the old woman who was still calling them names and accusing them of desecrating their holy Sigil.

"We would do nothing of the sort!" Amara rebutted firmly. Emrys frowned, he was hoping for a different response.

Amara gave him little chance to say anything before jumping in again, "...wait Sigil? This is *the* Sigil of the Omniscient?" She turned to Emrys with furious eyes.

Feeling like her trust had been betrayed, like Emrys had convinced her to unknowingly touch a religious artifact, Amara had no words to express herself. She took a step toward Emrys who promptly took a step back.

"Did I forget to mention that?" Emrys said in a mischievous tone. As he cautiously stepped away from them both, Amara turned away and started walking. "You're going the wrong way," he explained.

Stopping in her tracks, Amara glared at Emrys and waited for him to point in the right direction. He lowered his head and gestured in the direction of the setting sun. It wasn't long before she was marching off and headed back towards Harvest. Storming off with heavy feet, Amara said nothing more to Emrys. Despite his best efforts to break the tension between them, he knew that this was going to be a long walk home for everyone.

Chapter 09

The small mining huts that surrounded Harvest paled in comparison to the grand house that stood at the highest point, near the town center. Amara's new home was bought and paid for by the UMI and they spared no expense for its first owner. It seemed almost out of place compared to the small but functional huts that made up most of the residential areas.

These small iron huts were nothing to admire but the walls were deceptively thick which helped to normalize the temperature and cancel outside noises. If it were not for the automated shutters that opened at the same time every morning it would have been difficult to know the time of day from inside. For the residents of Harvest, the changing of seasons did not help to stabilize their internal clocks either. It was a slow morning for Emrys but he eventually found his way to the door.

With a slight yawn, Emrys stepped out of his hut and into a surprisingly cool morning. It was a sure sign that Fall was beginning to show itself. The few sparse trees that decorated the town were beginning to change but most of the evergreens stood firm as they always did.

It was a welcome change for Emrys to have such a short summer season. He thought to himself that perhaps he would be as lucky with Amara, perhaps he could gain her trust again. The short summer was a sign of good luck to those in Harvest, a superstition that Emrys would gladly accept if it improved his chances with her.

Before he could agonize more about his mistakes, Emrys quickly set out to meet his father. It was going to be another long day at the mines and he knew better than to be late. A small commuter tram had been built in the short time that the UMI had occupied Serec. It was one of many construction projects that the UMI had donated to Harvest as a show of good faith and support. Many people on Harvest resisted the change at first, but quickly accepted the luxuries that the UMI had to offer. Unsurprisingly, the tram only ran between Harvest and main dig site that was about ten miles away. Barely catching the tram as it departed for another round trip to the dig site, Emrys squeezed through the closing doors and quickly found a seat in the empty space inside.

On his way to the dig site, Emrys could feel the breeze blowing through the windows that were barely cracked open. He opened the window next to his seat a little more before sinking into the hardback chair. The steady shuffle of the tram that navigated the plotted course was enough to put him to sleep if it had not been such a short ride.

The jerking motion of the tram as it stopped at the site was enough to jolt Emrys' consciousness. Once he stepped off, Emrys watched as the automated tram shut its doors and turned back to town. It would return every hour until the last call at sunset.

Navigating through the large field of machinery that was scattered throughout the site, Emrys made his way to the main entrance. The entrance was a gaping tunnel that was carved into the side of a rocky ledge. Wide tire tracks littered the opening where machinery had made frequent trips in and out of the site. Disposing of blasted debris was a constant cycle that only stopped when something was broken.

As the lead engineer in the group, Emrys was responsible for keeping every piece in working order. The fact that no dumpers were coming or going was a bad sign, something had likely broken in the first shift. Emrys was glad to have caught that last tram or else he would have gotten an ear full for not being here to fix the problem. Inside the cave-like opening, he could hear voices yelling back and forth. The sound of machines running idle was overpowering, but Emrys was used it by now. He grabbed a hardhat and hearing protection then headed down the tunnel with a brisk pace.

"The damn laser cutters are sputtering out again!" a familiar voice barked over the deafening rattle of unstable pistons. Cole, Emrys' father was standing over the laser cutter that looked to be shaking off of the guidance rails that held it in place.

"You have to keep the..." Emrys replied with a sigh. He stopped to shut down the cutter before speaking again. It was going to be a long day and the last thing he needed was his throat to go hoarse in the first hour. "You have to keep the filters closed when you are cutting. It will open on its own and exhale when the heat builds."

Emrys knew his words were falling on deaf ears since his father was likely not the person to have mistreated the equipment. It was the third time this week that he had to tell someone how to maintain the machinery, though it was hard to blame anyone for not caring. Most of the crew was working for very little pay and morale was low. It had been over a decade since Cole had promised pay dirt and the UMI had only recently stepped in when some of the samples had shown a desirable concentration of Dust.

Dust, after all, was the reason for being on Serec and especially in the more hostile regions where Harvest was founded. It was the reason for Cole and his family to uproot their lives on Earth and make their way onto the frontier. A 50 kilogram load of this raw mineral could earn enough to feed a family for a year, and Cole risked everything to come here and see that happen.

Cole was a shorter but rugged looking man, wearing tattered coveralls and a hardhat. The gruff beard that painted his face was a foreshadowing of the voice to match and his leathery sun-baked skin was a battle scar of a long life of hard labor. Cole looked as if he was much older than he was, but he still had a quick wit and an even shorter temper. Most people knew better than to cross him, even on a good day. But he still seemed to have his reasons for being different to Emrys and his renowned temper was hardly ever an issue around his son. The same could hardly be said for Emrys however.

"Dad, you have to get another engineer. I'm not going to be here forever you know," Emrys threatened, though his tone was soft and more concerned.

"What are you talking about? This is why we came here!" Cole pressed the issue like it was an age old argument. His tone was dismissive, like he barely heard what Emrys was trying to tell him.

"Do you really want to get into this again? I see you for two minutes and it has already come to this," Emrys spoke with a rising voice. Each word seemed to grow louder and more aggressive. "This was your dream, not mine. If we had still been on Earth..."

"...we would have been hungry and living in the toxic streets. Harvest is my legacy to you, son." Cole interrupted.

"...at least we would have been together on Earth, at least *she* would have been alive!" Emrys could feel the frustration bubbling up inside of him. Often a gentle soul, it only took his father to send him to the edge. He clenched his fists and waited eagerly for a response, any excuse that he could throw back in his fathers' face. Emrys was ready for a fight. And the morning started out so peacefully.

"Your mother wanted this as much as I did..."

"...no, she wanted you to be happy; she supported you. There is a difference between following your dream and supporting someone else's." Emrys was talking about more than just his mother now, they both knew that. They both knew that it was not Emrys' dream to mine on Harvest. The argument started to feel like the same old routine for them both and it grew suddenly quiet.

Cole said nothing. He calmly walked to a makeshift bench that rested against the jagged walls of the cave. Grabbing a thermos that was lying nearby, he opened the lid and took a deep breath of the aroma inside. Emrys immediately recognized it as Coles' favorite thermos. After pouring a small serving into the lid Cole sat and stared at it, as if questioning if he even wanted to drink it.

"What's in the cup..." Emrys was still angry but his tone was more judgmental than spiteful.

"Why do you care? You are not going to be here forever; remember?" Cole replied in a mocking voice. He looked back down to his short drink and swirled it in circles, stirring it around.

"What's in the cup, Dad?" Emrys repeated himself, this time more assertive.

"You know that I quit that," Cole defended himself with every word. It was easy to see that he did not appreciate the sudden accusations that his son was raising.

Emrys rushed in and slapped the lid away from Cole, who barely moved. A small part of the hot liquid sprayed on his hand. *It was hot*, he thought to himself, a surprising discovery. Emrys smelled the spray on his hands and tasted it with the tip of his tongue.

"Are you happy?" asked Cole. "You just wasted a perfectly good cup of hydroponic Earth-grown tea. There is something about the gravity there that makes the leaves easier to brew." Cole rolled his eyes as he said, "A gift from our friends in the UMI." Emrys could see that his father was being sarcastic about the kind words he had for the UMI, but the rest was true. It was only tea.

Emrys felt sheepish but his pride would not let it be seen. He was still angry with Cole but already began to forget why he was so angry. Watching the lid roll to a stop, Emrys could see the last of the tea spill from the lid. With the cleanest part of his shirt that he could find, Emrys picked up the lid and wiped it dry. Letting out a heavy sigh, he quietly placed the lid onto the makeshift bench and quietly walked away.

"You may always have a reason to be angry but you'll never have a reason to doubt me," Cole yelled out to his son who faded into the darkness of the cave.

"You always hear that blood is thicker than water but they never tell you that it is twice as bitter," a voice echoed nearby.

The voice came from a shadowing figure that stood between Cole and the bright light from the cave entrance. With only his silhouette to give away his identity, Cole struggled to adjust his eyes to the blinding light that waited just outside. Slowly his eyes focused and the shadowing figure took shape.

"Colonel Miles Binson, what brings you out here to the mines?" Cole was only being polite, knowing that the Colonel only made business calls, never personal ones.

"My superiors tell me that the latest soil samples are turning up some very positive results. I think it's time we discuss what the UMI can do for you." Miles was so smug with his words that even Cole took notice.

"So... It is time to pay the Piper as they say," Cole spoke in his usual gruff monotone. Between the conversation he was having with his son and one he was about to have with the Colonel, things just kept going from bad to worse.

Chapter 10

The cooling breeze that blew across the plains struck Amara as a welcome change. The summer season was harsh but somehow more pleasant than the extreme heating and cooling that Earth had been experiencing over the last century. The extreme changes were all that she knew and the subtle shift in weather in Harvest warmed her heart.

She took one last breath of clean air, something that she was still growing accustom to, before stepping into the Harvest Mencist Academy. It was strange to be back in the familiar setting of an academy but feel more alien than ever. Things were clearly not the same as the academy that she had attended for nearly two decades.

The walls had a faint aroma of fresh paint and the equipment throughout the facility appeared to be nearly unused. The halls were scarce with people and the building felt larger than the population required. It was clear to Amara that the UMI was expecting substantial growth in the coming years. It was also a stark contrast to the aging facility in her home city.

On Earth, her academy was a building that looked and felt as cold and uninviting as a state prison. In Harvest, the colors were warm and welcoming and the people were serious but somehow less frigid or void of expression. Sharing a chuckle, two female cadets crossed her path as they shared in some personal story that Amara could not quite hear through the whispers.

"Excuse me," one of the girls said as they crossed in front of Amara. She looked up to Amara and smiled politely.

The girl appeared to be a student at the academy but her warm personality did not match Amara's expectation. Clumsily pressed against the young girl's chest was her tablet, issued by each UMI academy to every student of deserving age. It was their bible, their lifeline to the outside world; something that Amara knew quite well. The screen was still on and displayed a number of high level mathematics and logistics books, a welcome sight for Amara. At least their education was up to her standards, but still, the young girl's smile looked so real.

Amara wondered if the girl had a gift for trained expressions or if she genuinely intended to smile, as if her mind and her heart were in synch. Pretending not to notice, Amara did not return the smile; she only waited until the two young girls crossed before she continued down the hall.

Amara questioned the atmosphere as a place for learning, certainly as a place to raise a Mencist. In her eyes it felt more like a nursery than a military facility. It was clear that the culture and people of Harvest had a strong influence on the aesthetics of the building. Thinking back to the young girls that crossed her path, the warm aesthetics appeared to infect the personalities of the students as well. She began to question if the teachings would measure up to her standard, though her intelligences scores often tipped the scales on Earth, making her judgment a bit unbalanced for the common student populous.

It did not take much effort to find the main offices just beyond the foyer. They were located to the left of the main center hall. Long panes of glass separated the offices from the hallway. Amara could see two glass doors with large polished metal handles near the center of the large stretch of glass windows. The open layout of desks and chairs inside was a perfect arrangement that allowed natural light to pass throughout the office space.

With her documents in hand, Amara waited to be noticed just inside the office entrance. It did not take long for the receptionist to see her standing there. The receptionist was a middle-aged woman with dark hair and naturally brown skin. Her motherly smile and slightly shabby demeanor was a suitable fit for her shapely figure that told Amara some history about the woman.

Amara deduced that the woman likely had a child. One... No, two children, and she took more pride in her work than her appearance. Amara did not have enough information to continue digging into the womans' past and she quickly abandoned the Mencist analysis. Even after a summer long lapse in her teachings, she realized that old habits were hard to break. She promptly handed the papers to the woman who was now waiting with her hand extended.

"Thank you," said the woman as she gentle took the documents from Amara's hand. She spent a few minutes browsing the papers.

For a moment, the womans' eyes widened and she quickly closed the small stack of papers. Perhaps there was information that she was not meant to know. It was yet another expression that Amara refused to analyze.

"If you'd like to wait there," said the woman. She kindly pointed to a row of chairs that rested against the glass panels, "Mr. Scates will be with your shortly."

Amara sat down and placed her carryall in the seat beside her. The faint sounds of music could be heard from one of the desks and the subtle tapping of keys was a constant drone that was overpowered by the rare sound of a door opening or closing. Voices would frequently erupt, but in a low whisper, as neighboring workers would banter about some form of daily news or message that they had just received. The atmosphere was eerie in some ways for Amara, a person who was more accustomed to the bustling sounds of an Earthan city academy.

"Mrs. Agemy, send in the visitor please," a voice called out from a private office just behind the receptionist.

"Mr. Scates will see you now," said Mrs. Agemy. She kindly pointed to the door and waited for Amara to pass before escorting her to the door.

Amara stepped inside and took the first seat nearest to her, placing her carryall on her lap. From her seat she could see all of the shelves that lined the back wall and the dark cherry wood desk that separated her from the academy Dean. The small office was suffocating her with mounds of old books in underutilized spaces. It was an obvious attempt to replicate a historic time but seemed more wasteful than poignant to Amara.

Mr Scates was an elder man with salt and pepper hair and olive skin. Though he wore it comfortably, his formal clothing was likely a uniform required by his position. He rested back in his chair to meet her eyes and welcomed her into the office. Amara barely had time to introduce herself before Scates jumped in.

"I've been expecting you." Scates greeted her with a warm smile. He quickly took the documents that Mrs. Agemy had already extended to him. Mrs. Agemy promptly walked back to her desk and could be heard typing memos and filing papers.

"Tell me your honest assessment of Mrs. Agemy," inquired Scates. The subtle scratches in his voice gave every word a sense of weight and importance. Amara could easily see that it was not difficult for him to demand respect amongst the staff at the academy.

"She is married and has two children. She greatly enjoys her work but would rather be home with her family. Other factors tell me that her husband must be alive and well, but is making very little or no money at all.

Her story is not too uncommon and thus easily categorized," concluded Amara.

"Impressive," said Scates with a smile. "And, in a word, what would you say to describe my office?"

"Old," she promptly replied. Perhaps a more gentle word would have sufficed but her mouth seemed to move more quickly than her thoughts. An eruption of laughter from Mr Scates followed her description.

"Though it was more literal than I was expecting, you are correct. The intension of this design is to remind myself of what we are trying to do at this academy." Scates stood to his feet and walked to the entrance of his private office. "Walk with me," he said.

Amara gave a slight nod and followed Scates out of the offices and into the main hall. They proceeded to drift through the academy and discuss the philosophies of the school. Along the way, Scates would stop and use one of the classes in session to describe the differences in what Harvest was attempting to accomplish.

"So you see," he said. "We have very capable students here, Mencists who we have cultivated in an environment that has been deemed more suitable for human learning."

"Deemed by whom exactly," asked Amara in a suspicious tone.

"I can see that you have doubts," he proposed. Scates paused for a moment. He appeared to be struggling to find the words but quickly returned to the conversation, "You did come here for employment opportunities, correct?" Scates waited for a response and Amara only nodded in return.

"I would like to extend to you a job offer," he said plainly.

"For how long," asked Amara.

"You would stay for a trial of one full year, at which point you are free to stay or leave. I am certain that there are a number of government branches that would pull strings to have you in their circles." Scates was direct and Amara appreciated his candor.

"I see," Amara continued to reply in a somewhat suspicious tone. She paused for a moment to study his posture and the subtle shifting of his weight from leg to leg. Everything that she saw implied that he was extending an honest hand to her.

"I can understand if you are reluctant to accept. Your intelligences records are the exception and frankly you could go anywhere and probably make more money. Why would you stay here of all places," asked Scates. His genuine curiosity was apparent but Amara did not feel comfortable discussing personal matters with him.

"I have my reason," was her only reply.

"The truth is this; every UMI vessel that stops at Harvest is leaving more and more troops behind. These soldiers are forming families and we are expecting an influx of military students in the next two to five years..."

"It sounds like this small mining town is becoming a military waypoint." Amara's curiosity was peaked.

If what the man had said was true, it would mean that the UMI was using Serec -- specifically Harvest -- as a waypoint, a tactical stopping place for long distance warfare. Amara knew that mobilizing troops from Serec would be much faster than the decade long journey from Earth to the outer reaches.

"You may be right about that, and it would be a great opportunity if they did," Scates argued. He was clearly trying to entice Amara to accept the offer, hoping that she would enjoy her work enough to turn down the inevitable offers to come.

Once the UMI fabricated a permanent station in Harvest, they would likely be recruiting any capable body in the area. A resident Mencist with topnotch intelligences records would be a sure thing for an officer's position. It would not hurt Amara's chances that she was the daughter of a well decorated Colonel here in Harvest.

"...and you want me to help teach a group of cadets who are only a few years younger?" Amara asked. She made a strong argument. It would be difficult, though not impossible, to command a class of people barely younger than herself.

Scates chuckled at her implications, "You would be starting with early-grade cadets and moving up with them. I think that you have something to teach the younger generation of Mencist in Harvest and maybe they have a thing or two to teach you as well."

Amara accepted his proposal after Scates stated many convincing facts. As the daughter of a decorated Colonel, Amara had already shown signs of an expert Mencist. She would not have lasted long on Serec before the UMI would send her back to Earth. Now, she would be employed by a government sanctioned facility which implied immediate denial of an early draft; at least until her annual contract was expired. If her suspicions were true, by that time, a station would have been built in Harvest. She would be free to renew her contract or enlist for an officer's rank within the Harvest military station.

A job within the ranks of UMI might have made her father proud but Amara had other plans. For the first time in her life she was beginning to feel like there may be a friend in her future. There was no sentiment in her thoughts, only curiosity. Having a friend, a companion, would certainly be a valuable lesson in learning more about human nature. At least that was her way of rationalizing her decision to stay in Harvest.

Amara eventually said her goodbyes and left the academy for the day. Her job would be effective as of tomorrow morning at 0800 hours. Making her way off of the campus, she found herself steering back toward the town center. It was strange; it seemed like every time she stepped outside and started walking, Amara would end up in the town center before long. Maybe it was the circular design of the town and the flow of the streets. Perhaps it might have been one of the first places that she met Emrys and felt drawn to it. Either way, the town center was where her thoughts were taking her.

She decided to spend the rest of her day watching the people pass by. The town center was easily the busiest place in Harvest and served as the hub for many pedestrians going to work or looking for a bite to eat. Amara wanted to further study the culture on Harvest. It was familiar because everyone still expressed common human tendencies but different because they appeared less guarded than any place on Earth that she had seen.

After some searching, she located a bench that stood on its own. The bench was on the center of a small pedestrian overpass that connected two open-design buildings. It was a perfect place to oversee most of the town center and it looked to be a good place to watch the sun set behind the taller structures. Though Amara enjoyed the low rumbles of the distant crowd, she was not alone for long.

An elder woman slowly wobbled up to the bench. She kindly gestured to the bench as if to ask if anyone else had been sitting with her. Amara shook her head and shifted further to one side to make room. Together, they sat there quietly for some time and Amara would occasionally shift her eyes to sneak a peek at the elder woman.

The elder woman barely moved and had her eyes closed more often than not. She was not sleeping, only basking in the late-day sun, enjoying whatever fleeting moments she may have had. When she did open her eyes, Amara could see that they were white as snow. She wondered how the elder woman could sense the world since her eyes had clearly failed her long ago.

"I don't believe I have seen you here before," said the elder woman. She continued to look forward with her eyes barely open. Amara found her poor choice of words to be ironic for a blind woman.

"No. I have only been in Harvest for a season now. My name is Amara," she replied quietly. Amara was only half attentive as she continued to study the people below. Her hand was unknowingly clenched around the glass locket of seeds around her neck.

"Amara... What a beautiful name," the elder woman said. As she smiled, her eyes seem to disappear even more. "What are you holding in her hands," she inquired.

Yet again the elder woman surprised Amara. She questioned if she had misread the elder woman or was being deceived. No, the woman was most definitely blind. Pondering the possibilities, Amara thought that she must have had some form of sensory augmentation, but Amara could not see if it was biomedical or something else completely. The woman's hands were free, gently crossed on her lap, and she did not seem to be making any awkward twitches or gestures that would imply biomedical assistance.

"They are seeds from Earth. The sands here appear to be saturated in salts and the environment is too hostile for Earthan wildflowers to thrive. I keep it only as a memory." Her final words were warm and surprisingly emotion. Amara surprised herself at how easily she would offer something so personal. Her attention on the crowds slowly faded as she became more engaged with the woman beside her.

The elder woman chuckled lightly and said, "If you show a bit of diligence and even a little faith, you might be surprised. Faith is something that we often attribute to religion but they are not one in the same. You don't have to be religious to have faith in something beyond your knowing."

Amara pondered on that statement. For a Mencist, not knowing or having an inability to reach a logical reason meant that it was a statistical improbability. Faith was not something they taught at the academy. "Do you believe in the Rector?" she asked.

"If I told you, would it change the way you feel?" The elder woman answered with a question, but did not appear to wait for Amara's response.

Amara did not reply and assumed that the question was meant to be rhetorical. It would have only satisfied her curiosity to know of the elder woman's beliefs. They both smiled and continued to overlook the thinning crowd below, but only for a short while. The elder woman slowly stood to her feet and quietly walked away, barely unnoticed. Amara never did know her name.

Several minutes later, Amara could feel the chilling wind start to rise and the day glow begin to fade. Now that the summer season was over the skies were much darker than the diffused light that she had seen for most of her nights in Harvest. The chill only served to remind Amara that she was alone on that bench and the words of the elder woman somehow had more weight to them now.

She questioned if her reaction to Emrys and his stunt with the Sigil was more than it should have been. Maybe it was an overreaction; perhaps she should have shown a little faith in him and listened to what he was trying to say. They had not spoken to each other since that day and Amara felt the blame. With high hopes, she convinced herself to make amends soon, if not tomorrow.

Chapter 11

"So... It is time to pay the Piper as they say," Cole spoke in his usual gruff monotone.

Both Cole and Miles stood quietly and watched as Emrys faded into the darkness of the cave. Reaching into his pocket, Miles shuffled to the side and pulled out a small pollutant barrier before attaching it to his septum. The fine mineral particles in the air were too much for his senses and he wiggled his nose to try and keep from sneezing. Looking back into the darkness of the cave, Miles wondered how potent the smell must have been at the furthest depths.

"Children are a strange thing. They bring out of best and worst in us." Ignoring Cole's earlier comment, Miles had a ponderous tone. He smiled gently, as if he was thinking of his own daughter and their sometimes troubled history. Miles adjusted the barrier once more before speaking again. "Alas, I did not come to chat entirely about our future generation."

"Of course," replied Cole, "Let's meet in my office. It will get you out of the mineral mist." They both strolled out of the cave and into a small trailer that sat nearby.

The trailer was a shanty space but it was a serviceable place for blueprints, machine schematics, and other important documents. Across the room, a small wooden desk that appeared to be fabricated from scraps of construction material decorated the corner of the office.

Various maps were pinned onto the walls of the office, each one detailing a sector of the underground passages.

The maps were so many and so detailed that Miles was lost in them, trying to follow some sort of logical path. It was impossible for him to understand the flow of the maps. It appeared as if a city had been erected underneath the surface of Serec.

"They look like drawings of an ant farm." Miles described the maps with a chuckle in his voice. He traced his fingers along the fine lines that looked to have the precision of an architectural building plan. Near the top, the document was labeled 'Section 9' and was crossed out with a red marker.

"You might say that. We had to close Section 9 last year when we dug too close to an aquifer. They didn't have a chance..." Cole's tone quickly turned somber.

Cole lost many good people in Section 9 and it clearly still weighted heavily on his heart. He struggled for a brief moment to maintain his composure. Emrys had been working in Section 9, early that day, and that map was a reminder of how close his son came to an early grave. More recently, Section 9 had been used to pump water into the machinery as part of the coolant systems.

"I visit Section 9 every morning. Without their efforts we might have quit on this site a long time ago," continued Cole. He knew that, without clean water to run the cutters and diggers, the project would have come to a halt. He was forever indebted to them, more than they would ever know.

"My condolences," said Miles in a seemingly unsympathetic tone. He placed a small tablet on the desk in front of Cole. The tablet contained the Continued Contract Agreement between Hughend Co. and the UMI. It was a renewal of the contract that the UMI had made to fund the project and purchase the findings.

Cole carefully read through the agreement. A lot had changed, likely due to the recent success of finding Dust mineral depots. They were getting much closer to finding a large deposit and the UMI knew that. Upon inspection, he read a slew of non-standard agreements. There was a non-compete clause that prevented the sale of goods to other clients, followed by a change in profit shares. It appeared that, as Hughend Co. produced larger quantities of Dust the UMI would receive a larger share of profits.

The percentages were inexact and floated from number to number, all of them tied to stipulations. It would ensure that Cole and his staff would be profitable while still relying on the assistance of the UMI. Living so far out in the frontier meant that Cole had no choice but to agree to the unreasonable demands. Sickened by every word, Cole knew that they would forever depend on the support of the UMI. Every paragraph that Cole read seemed to enrage him even more. He watched each sentence slowly take more and more of his life's work away from him. Helpless to do little more than continue reading, he clenched the tablet tightly in his hands until the screen twitched and the alloy frame creaked.

In a flash, Cole pulled a small bowed knife from its belted sheath. He pushed Miles against the wall and held him there tightly with his forearm on Miles' chest, and with the same hand, the blade against his throat. They said nothing for moment and only Cole's heated breathing could be heard, escaping his lips. A gust of wind blew through the rickety trailer door, a noise that helped to break the still silence of the room. Whenever Miles threatened to shuffle or move, Cole pushed him back against the wall even harder.

"Are you trying to cheat me out of my legacy," asked Cole in a low and threatening whisper. His eyes never left Miles and his blade was so close that it creased against Miles' skin when he breathed.

"It looks like you are trying to do that all by yourself. Do you know what the UMI does to a civilian who assaults a ranked officer? Tsk-tsk Mr. Hughend, I expected better." Miles was calm and almost seemed to enjoy the violent gesture. He knew better than to smile in the face of an angry man like Cole but his confidence in the situation was undeniable.

Cole slowly eased the pressure of the knife and stabbed it into the table. He slowly sank into the chair that sat at his desk and gave Miles one last stern gaze. With a long sigh, he stared at the tablet once more and grazed over the stream of numbers with lifeless eyes. Cole rubbed his chin as if he was deep in thought, as if he was debating on whether to call their bluff. In the end, he closed his eyes, clenched his jaw, and reluctantly swiped his wrist across the tablet. The faint blue flash of the screen let them know that the transaction was complete.

With the blade away from his throat, Miles continued, "I am willing to overlook this because I like you. I like what you've done for us these many years. You have a unique opportunity to be a hero, a pioneer for the next generation of human evolution..."

"...cut the crap," interrupted Cole in a spiteful voice. "You want the mineral Dust for your cellular augmentation project, but science only garners the UMI's grace when it benefits them. I might be a miner but that doesn't make me an idiot, so stop treating me like one."

"Have a good day Cole," Miles replied. "It has been a pleasure doing business with you. I am sure we will see each other again real soon." The wiry grin on his face was unmistakable and it only served to irritate Cole further. Extending his hand to Cole, Miles waited, but a handshake was never returned.

"Watch that first step," Cole said in a flat voice as he leaned back in his chair and waited for Miles to leave.

Staring at the extended hand, he only nodded his head as politely as he could before gesturing a nod to the door.

Cole watched the rickety door ease shut as Miles walked out of the trailer and headed to the tram stop. He dragged his arm across the desk in frustration, clearing the table top. Sinking back into his chair, Cole slowed his breathing. Staring at the pile of scattered papers that were thrown to the floor, a partially covered photo of his wife could be seen among them. He carefully lifted the photo and brushed the mineral deposits and other debris off of her face.

"Did I do the right thing Meyra," Cole asked of his late wife. He sat in silence and waited for an answer that never came.

Chapter 12

Another sleepless night had passed for Emrys, one of many in the recent weeks. He couldn't help but agonize over his missteps. *I should have been more forward with her,* he thought to himself. Masking the truth about the Sigil was childish, even if he had the best of intensions. Admittedly not all of his intensions were pure. Emrys was hoping to woo her with excitement and maybe win her heart in a brief moment of weakness. Alas, his own awkwardness once again tripped him when courage was what he really needed.

"...I am so awkward..." he mumbled to himself. The late morning sun crept in through the iron shutters and slits of thin bright light filled the room. It was a constant reminder of what he told himself would happen today, he would make his feelings known.

Emrys was slow to prepare for the day. His usual speedy pace was reduced to a sloth's sense of urgency. He was clearly procrastinating out of fear; fear of rejection, or perhaps fear of simply knowing the truth. Questioning what her response might be, Emrys did not know if he had the strength to accept her kind of rejection. Amara had a special way of turning the blade in his heart, and kind words were seldom in her vocabulary. Since childhood, he had strong feelings for Amara and a strong need to protect her. It was something that only he knew, and today was the day that it would all change.

The thought of Amara on Earth, in their childhood, tickled the scars in his arm. He clenched his fist in and out many times until the numbness was gone. The waking mornings were always the worst for him. When his arm lay still for too long, as it did in his sleep, it seemed to grow stiff and his forearm ached with sharp pains. It felt more like pins and needles than the soreness tired muscles.

After his slow morning, Emrys made his way to the Binson home in hopes to confront Amara. He was fully prepared for Amara's sharp tongue to give him a lashing or two. He thought of it as one of her better traits and only wanted them to be on speaking terms again. Though he would have wanted more by now, Emrys admitted that his mistakes may have tarnished their friendship.

Pausing to track his course, Emry made a mental note of how to reach Amara's house. The fastest route to her house would be to follow the beltway along the town and avoid the town center, where most people crossed on their way to work. Emrys walked at a brisk pace, much faster than he usually did. His nerves were almost pushing him, urging him to get it over with. Once the tall house was in plain view Emrys slowed his heart and his narrowed his stride. He thought that it would be wise not to show up sweating and panting, recalling the many times that Amara had criticized him for that.

At the door, Emrys was paralyzed. He had convinced himself to come this far but had done nothing to prepare what he wanted to say. He slowly inhaled and took his last deep breath to calm his nerves once more before knocking on the door. Only seconds later, he began to question if it was smart to come here.

Before Emrys had a chance to turn away, the sound of door hinges caught his attention. The door gentle crept open and Miles was standing there in civilian clothes. It was off-putting at first; Emrys had never seen Miles in anything other than his military uniform. He was also expecting Amara to answer the door and was instead greeted by this menacing figure. Emrys stumbled with his words for a moment but eventually regained his composure.

"Hello Colonel. I was wondering if I could speak with Amara," Emrys said in a polite tone. His eyes were focused slightly down and his head was turned somewhat to the side. He had trouble meeting Miles, eye to eye but he struggled to do so.

"Come in," replied Miles with confident grin. Miles gestured to the left of the door where an arched entrance welcomed them both into the next room.

The room was fashioned much like a den, though most of the walls were still bare. Emrys could see a few pieces of temporary furniture and small end tables next to two chairs. The lack of permanent furniture told him that Miles spent little time in the house or had little time to decorate. The walls that were so simple and plain lacked a woman's touch, an eye for color and contrast. Though Amara had a feminine appearance, being a keeper of the house was not part of her academy training. The space was neat and organized which was to be expected for military housing, but it lacked the homely aesthetic of a place lived in, a place to call home. Emrys wondered if their home on Earth was similar to this or if it still carried the memories of Amara's mother.

"Would you like a cup of coffee?" asked Miles. But before Emrys could reply, Miles corrected himself, "You are probably a bit too young to appreciate coffee; I'll get you some tea."

Miles walked over to a small wet bar in the corner of the room. There was no alcohol in it, only a variety of coffees and teas. It was not surprising, given the lack of grain alcohol on Serec. Coffees and teas were the main staple of social drinking instead, though many coffees were genetically altered to give the same inebriated sensation as rum or vodka.

Placing a tea cup on the counter, Miles poured heated water over a distiller that was filled with loose leaves of tea. He dipped the distiller into the now colored water for one last steep before draining the leaves and dumping them into a disposal unit next to the bar. Emrys could already smell the aroma of the fine tea as Miles placed it on the end table next to his chair.

Emrys gently blew air over the top of the tea to cool the surface before taking a small but savory sip. It was the best that he had ever tasted and the fruity but tannic flavors tickled his tongue, seconds after he had swallowed. He was insulted at the gesture that Miles had made, implying that he was too young for coffee, but he still appreciated the fine tea that rested in his hands.

"She is not here I am afraid," Miles said in reply to Emrys' original question. "Amara is out running an errand for me." Miles spoke softly but in a polite and reasonable tone. Waiting for Emrys to reply, he eased back into his chair and sipped his cup quietly.

Emrys was surprised. Why had Miles invited him into his home and offered him fine teas, only to tell him that Amara was not there. Miles must have had an ulterior motive. Perhaps he intended to gain inside knowledge of the Dust mines. Maybe he just wanted to know the person who was spending so much time with his daughter.

"I... I want you to know that I do have a connection with Amara. I care about her, a lot. She..." Emrys slowly squeaked out a few words at a time. He struggled to maintain eye contact but managed to build the confidence for at least that much. His words seemed to fall on deaf ears as Miles quickly cut him short.

"She is beyond you," said Miles calmly. "She is destined for great things, and needs to be with a partner that is destined for great things."

Emrys immediately understood what Miles was trying to say. Emrys would live and die on this planet, and no one would remember his name. He was the son of a miner, be it a successful and renowned figure, the father of Harvest; but still a miner non-the-less. In a militarized society, he would be no better remembered than the rebels who stood against the UMI early in their history and lost.

If Emrys was going to gain his respect and earn his right to be with Amara, Emrys knew what he had to do. He knew that his only hope of being closer to Amara was to prove his worth in the only language that Miles understood. Emrys would have to serve his time with the UMI.

Serving for the UMI was something that Emrys had considered for many years but the loss of his mother put out any fire he had to protect the UMI. Her death only served to light a new fire of bitterness and hatred. He hated the UMI for what they had done but he quickly buried his feelings before replying to Miles, who was still awaiting a response.

"I will have to respectfully disagree with your assessment Colonel. I think you might be surprised by what I am capable of." Emrys spoke in a cool manor, one that could have easily been mistaken for the words of a Mencist. He calmly stood and walked to front door. "Thank you for the tea," he said; again in a dry and cold voice.

As Miles closed the door behind Emrys, a shuffling sound could be heard at the top of the stairs. Amara, in her bath rope, peeked out from around the corner. She gently dabbed her head to keep the freshly wet hair from dripping on the floor.

"Was someone at the door?" Amara asked. The clueless look on her face told Miles that she had not heard a word of their conversation.

Miles gave his daughter a warm smile and replied, "It was no one important."

Chapter 13

Emrys stepped off of the tram and stretched his legs. The sun still had that early morning glow that seemed to energize him on days like today. Bathing in the sun's light for a second, he was not especially motivated to dive into the cave once more. The darkness of the caves can weigh on a person after some time, and he had other things on his mind which did not help to lighten his mood.

The grounds just outside of the cave were barren but Emrys could hear the hoses rattling against their restraints. People were working down there but it was uncommon to see the site so serene. His immediate thought was that someone had broken another laser cutter, but the hoses would not be running and the generators would have shut down. No, this was something else. Cole must have called for all hands on deck.

Grabbing a hardhat and a tablet, he raced down the cave entrance. A faint sound of voices could be heard from Section 12. The further into the darkness he reached the louder the screams became. Emrys could feel his heart racing.

Cole, are you there? Emrys tried communicating with his data-link but there was no response. He knew that is was a slim chance; so many residents had stopped using them since Harvest was founded, and many of them had disabled their links by that point. But he had to try something, anything to find out what was going on.

As he ran down the darkened tunnels, Emrys kept an eye on his tablet. The beacons indicated the miners who still have functioning locators, or bothered to turn them on. There were locators everywhere, a lot of them. But most of the locators were concentrated in the main branch of the Section 12 hub.

Emrys trotted on until he reached his destination, panting and wheezing. The sounds of echoing screams took a more clear form now, and began to sound more like cheers. After catching his breath, he stopped to examine the area which had since been filled with men covered in white ash and cheering Cole's name. He had never seen a smile so wide or heard a laugh so loud from his father, not in a long time.

Emrys could barely hear Cole talking over the chatter of the men and the sounds of music playing from their tablets. Their loud voices echoed through the cave tunnels, making it difficult for Emrys to focus on his fathers' voice. He could only make out a few words between the lulls of the crowd and listened as Cole was thanking them all, but he had little more to say. The joy in his voice was overwhelming but the crowd that was erupting with laughter and cheers were quieted by a few short waves of Cole's hand.

"...and to the men and women of Section 9," Cole said in a more somber voice. The crowd of miners held up their pickaxes and wrenches, clanging them together like two ton glasses of champagne. The moment of silence was broken after Cole asked them to turn the music on again, and the party seemed to grow even louder than before.

Emrys watched his father step down and cut through to the crowd as they raced to meet each other. Cole was wide-eyed and looked strangely manic but Emrys dismissed his father's appearance. Today looked like a good day for them and he convinced himself that excitement was more and appropriate, whatever it may have been.

"We need to talk," Cole blurted out before Emrys could begin to ask why everyone was celebrating, though he had his suspicions. There was only one reason why they were in this hole in the ground, Dust.

Cole walked briskly out of the Section 12 hub and headed back towards the entrance. At nearly a jogging pace, Emrys was struggling to keep up. He could see that his father was still shaking from all of the excitement and the adrenaline that still ran through his veins. They didn't speak a word to each other since Emrys was having trouble to keeping up, still exhausted from his sprint into Section 12. He could only make out a few mumbling words from Cole's lips, whatever he managed to catch in the brief moments that they were side by side.

"...we'll need cutters... more men... radiant barrier containers, lots of containers...," Cole said. It was as if he was lost in thought, trying to make sense of the next big step that he needed to take. Cole had been digging for Dust for so long that he was nearly at a loss with what to do with it, now that he had found it.

They had finally reached the entrance and made their way into Cole's office. Cole grabbed a towel that was hanging over his chair and wiped the soot from his face before plopping into the chair. Emrys, reaching his limit of patience, paced back and forth in a nervous pattern.

"So, are you going to tell me what the heck is going on," asked Emrys after giving up on waiting for Cole to speak clearly.

"We did it son, oh man we did it," Cole replied with jubilation. "The moment we hit that mineral deposit I could feel it in my bones."

"I am really happy for you, Dad..."

"...for us!" interrupted Cole. The air was still for a moment. Still wide-eyed, Cole paused as if he was waiting for Emrys to agree with him, but Emrys did not. The ecstatic look on Coles face quickly turned to confusion. "What's going on here? This is what your mother and I have been promising you from the start."

"Dad, I don't want to get into this again. I have been waiting for this to happen; for you to have the money to hire a real engineer. Now that you have the money, I think it is a good time for me to leave..." Emrys was almost grave with his words. He knew that it would break his father's heart but he had been threatening to leave for years. It was only a matter of time and Emrys had hoped that his father would understand.

The room was silent for some time. Neither side wanted to pick up the verbal bomb shell that Emrys had laid on the table. They had been on Serec for over a decade and Emrys had spent most of those years at the dig site. He shadowed his father and, in turn, Cole taught him everything he knew. In Coles mind, there was no other outcome until today.

Finally, Cole broke the silence when he said, "I see," in a sedated tone, just before he sank deeper into his chair. Those two powerful words were the jagged little pills that Emrys had to swallow. They were the verbal confirmation from Cole, telling Emrys that he understood and had accepted what Emrys was saying.

Emrys felt a pain in his heart. He was hoping for Cole to say more, to yell at him and fight with him. Fighting was how they always communicated and now Cole appeared to have given up the fight before it began. It was uncharacteristic of Cole to be so passive and it made Emrys a little nervous. Perhaps Cole had always known and Emrys was the one who never followed through.

"Where will you go?" Cole asked.

"I don't know," Emrys replied in a quiet voice. "I am going to talk to a UMI recruiter. I am told that they..." Emrys wanted to justify his motivations. Cole hated the

UMI more than he did but Cole gave him little time to explain.

"...UMI!" Cole exclaimed with a snort in his voice. "All they do is take; they took most of this from us," he explained as he waved his hands around carelessly. Emrys knew that the contracts were being renegotiated but Cole never told him what had happened. From his comments, Emrys could only assume that things did not go well. "They took your mother and now they are taking you too..." Cole's voice now seemed as quiet and grave as Emrys was.

Each word that crossed Cole's lips was defeated, a very different tone from the man he had just met inside the caves. Emrys was beginning to question if now was the time to tell his father. He barely gave Cole a full day to enjoy the fruits of his labor before letting him know that he may be losing his son because of his success. Suddenly, it did not feel as right for Emrys to steal his only joyful moment in years, but it was too late to take his words back.

Both Cole and Emrys took a moment of silence for his mother. Cole hardly ever brought up Meyra, his wife. It was often Emrys who would drag her into their fights and it was moments like these that made him regret using her death as a device. Emrys knew that it was a sore spot for them both and Cole felt especially guilty for losing her so soon after arriving on Serec.

"...I should go," Emrys said in a quiet voice. Inching towards the rickety door, he left quietly, gently guiding the door from slamming shut as it often did.

Cole never replied, he didn't say a word as he watched his son walk to the tram stop just outside of the dig site. He continued to watch as his son right up to the moment that he stepped onto the tram and rode away.

Chapter 14

The short ride on the tram seemed to end minutes too soon for Emrys. It was the only opportunity he had to experience the sensation of speed in Harvest. He was only a child, living on Earth, when he got to feel the force of raw speed in the pit of his stomach. Emrys was a fan of the many bullet trains on Earth, and he rode them often. Now, he was forced to slow his pace to what felt like a crawl and this tram was his only release.

The lack of manufacturing facilities near Harvest made it almost impossible to afford mobile transportation, let alone high speed trains. Though it would have been possible to expand much earlier, Cole would not allow the pre-mature industrialization of Harvest. He made every effort to exclude the UMI colonization efforts and part of that was boycotting their union factories. Though his reasons for ignoring UMI support were selfish and spiteful, it may have been the one decision that helped to save Harvest in a time when other settlements were having an economic collapse.

Cole found a way to trade exclusively with other settlements and colonies on Serec, without UMI subsidies, and it worked. Their trade mechanisms were more organic than the many tiers of red tape and taxation that came from the ease of the UMI's formulaic approach. The trade routes that passed through Harvest, and the hundreds of other settlements, was not perfect however. Shipments were often delayed and there were never enough of all the things that the town needed, but they managed.

Emrys didn't know if it was wrong or right to turn away UMI assistance. In the end they managed to construct the tram, various military academies and residential facilities. They even managed to construct a space port, the only one on Serec. Though Cole did his best to remain autonomous from the UMI, it seemed inevitable that Harvest would be absorbed in time.

As he stepped away from the tram, Emrys could see a figure sitting on a far bench. Wearing a cloak and hood to help shield her from the chilling breeze, the woman remained with her arms crossed to bundle the cloak tighter against her skin. From her slender but shapely figure and the long strands of hair that escaped her hood, Emrys knew instantly that the mysterious person was a woman but that was all he could decipher. She slowly turned her head but quickly perked up when she saw Emrys. The woman said nothing and sat motionless, waiting for Emrys to approach.

To Emrys, she looked familiar but the shadows cast by her clothing seemed to occlude her face, enough to obscure her identity. Curious to know more about the shadowy figure, Emrys approached her cautiously. Noticing that Emrys was approaching, the woman promptly stood and lifted the hood off of her head. It was Amara who appeared to have been waiting for quite some time. Brushing the few grains of white sand from her lap, she rubbed her hands together to warm them before extending one of them to greet Emrys. Nervously extending his own, they awkwardly shook hands as if it were the first time they had met.

"...I've been looking for you," Amara said. Though she sounded like her usual apathetic self, Emrys could sense a hint of nervousness.

"I suppose we were looking for each other," he replied with a warm smile.

A gust of wind blew past, stirring up a spiral of sand. It was the only sound that helped to break the silence between them. They both stared at each other, waiting for the other to say something. They had not spoken for so long that it seemed they both had little to say.

"I..."

"I wanted..."

When they finally decided to speak it was nearly at the same time. Both Emrys and Amara stumbled over each others' words and he smiled politely, chuckling a little at the same time. That unconventional exchange was all they needed to break the tension. Amara eventually nodded, letting Emrys know that he had the stage to speak.

"I wanted to apologize," he said sheepishly. Before Amara could respond, Emrys continued, "I only meant to show you something special, something that few might live to see."

"...I over reacted," interrupted Amara as her eyes nervously shifted in every direction. Her voice warmed Emrys' heart; it had been too long. "I appreciate what you did and it inspired me to learn more about it. I am working at the academy now."

"I heard about you working at the academy but I wasn't sure," Emrys replied.

Amara was not lying about her research. She had spent many of her weeks apart from Emry, studying documents on the artifact near Harvest, the Sigil. Though there was little information to be had, most of it shrouded in religious context, Amara discovered many truths to what Emrys had originally told her on that day.

Many of the technological and biological advancements in the last millennia had been attributed to the discovery of the Sigil and other alien artifacts throughout the known universe. Amara quivered at the thought that the most recent advancements in human evolution were a product of plagiarism and not innovation. She questioned if the human race had reached their limit, or if their natural evolution had finally stagnated. If there was race of aliens still alive, who possessed this level of intelligence, she wondered what they would do; how they would react to humankind.

The pinging sounds of the tram's last call caught the attention of Emrys. He quickly peered up to the sky and saw that the day was not yet half over; he had plenty of time.

"Can I show you something," Emrys asked, to which Amara quietly nodded. He instinctively grabbed her hand and raced back to the tram.

Barely catching the door as it was closing, Emrys jumped inside with Amara in hand. Guiding her to a seat, he sat down next to her and they waited for the tram to begin its trek back to the dig site. He had not been this close to her in a long time, not since the day he took her to see the Sigil. Looking down, Emrys noticed that he was still holding her hand and nervously let go. Amara did not notice; she was busy looking at the white salt-stained dunes of sand that seemed to roll in the distance like waves of an ocean.

"You shouldn't stare for too long," Emrys reminded her again. "The white sands reflect a lot of the sun's rays. It was not uncommon for some of the early settlers to develop snow blindness."

Amara knew about the blindness, Emrys alone had warned her many times over but she felt drawn to gaze at its destructive beauty. It was a strange phenomenon, snow blindness in the middle of a barren land, but it was true. The stern warning from Emrys reminded her of the elder woman that she had met in the town center. She never did learn the elder woman's name but she could recall those frosted white eyes.

Amara wondered if the elder woman's fate was a result of the white sands of Harvest. She shut her eyes tightly and waited for the bright light to wash out of them. Slowly, the spots in her vision faded and Amara could feel them returning to their natural state. Shuttering at the thought of losing her sight, Amara vowed to be more careful. By the time she opened her eyes they had reached the dig site.

Emrys stood up and gentle waved his hands toward the door, letting Amara pass and exit the tram first. He pointed to site and the cave entrance before walking in that direction. Something was different this time. Emrys could feel his hand trembling and his heart racing. He had told his father that he was leaving and has now found himself back on the site, in the same day.

Crossing by his father's trailer, Emrys could see a familiar figure standing in the window, staring back at them. Emrys only nodded his head in the direction of the trailer and held one finger up. The person inside gentle tipped their hardhat to acknowledge him. It was definitely Cole but he did not come out to greet them and Emrys did not stop.

Looking at the confused expression on Amara's face, Emrys had few words to say. "That was my dad," he explained in a quiet voice. He barely gave her time to question what had just happened before handing her a hardhat and marching into the cave.

"Do we need one of those," Amara asked as she pointed to a table full of tablets.

Noticing that one of the tablets had been left enabled and was displaying a grid of maps, she concluded that it was likely a schematic of the tunnels. The immense size and complexity of what little parts she could see made her nervous, and Amara knew that an untrained person could be lost forever in these depths. As far as she knew, it may have already happened at least once.

"We won't be going very far," he replied.

They walked until it was almost too dark for Amara to see. Stumbling on a few loose stones that rolled under her feet, she caught herself on Emrys to keep from falling. Emrys, once again, instinctively held her hand and guided her through the remainder of the path.

"Your eyes will adjust soon, I promise." Emrys' tone was warm and comforting.

Though his words were kind, it was a stark contrast to the feel Amara had when she held his hand. He was anxious about something and Amara wondered if it had something to do with what he wanted to show her. Waiting patiently, she knew that her questions would soon be answered.

"I feel like I've always known so much about you," he said, "and I took you to the Sigil for you to know something about Harvest. Now I wanted to share with you, a part of me."

Just over their heads, Amara could see a placard that read, *Section 1*. Below it, in smaller letters, there were only a few words engraved; *For Meyra*. Emrys took her hand and walked through the archway that held the cave walls in place. Once inside, Amara could see a large hollow that might have been a square kilometer in size. A massive reflecting pond consumed the center of the hollowed space and a dim light appeared to caustically illuminate every wall and ceiling. The light radiated from the water and colored the room in shades of green and blue. It was magnificent and it left Amara speechless.

"Meyra was my mother," Emrys quietly explained. "This is her resting place. My dad closed this sector soon after she died."

"Why did he close this one?" Amara asked. Though the scenery was beautiful, at first it seemed like an arbitrary choice.

"I'm not entirely sure why he chose this one. I suppose it was because she had chosen this place to start digging. It felt like the right thing to do, to give her the first site. My dad stopped all work in Section 1 after she passed away and started another branch."

"Your father sounds like a caring man," she said.

Amara was at a loss for words. A lifetime of apathy left her poorly equipped to comfort Emrys at a time like this. She turned her gaze from the shimmer underground waters to him, but only for a moment. With her eyes better adjusted to the dim lights, Amara could see him looking out, over the watery grave. She looked at him long enough to see an intensity in his eyes before turning away. Pretending not to notice his expressions, her attention returned to the pond.

"He was, and then he wasn't." Emrys paused, as if to reflect on the actions of his father. "He drank a lot, too much. It nearly killed him and me on more than one occasion. My life hasn't been perfect. I hope that you can live with that," said Emrys. His words were less of a question and more in the form of a statement. He wanted to let her know that some things in his life can never change, like his past.

"My mother left us because she was a kind and loving person who lived in a house with a sociopathic militant husband and a Mencist daughter who could not return her affection. I hope you can live with that," she replied.

Emrys smiled, but it was a peculiar one. It was almost a painful smile, like he had done so out of pity. It irritated Amara to see that awkward smile again. She could see through it so easily and yet he still continued to humor her with that painful grin.

"Are you mocking me again," asked Amara.

"I am not sure if I should laugh or cry at a story like that. But if you meant to lighten my mood, you may have succeeded," Emrys said with a chuckle.

Emrys did not notice that he had been holding her hand since they walked into the hollow. He froze for a moment and questioned what he should do. Eventually he decided to ease his grip and slowly pull away. "I'm sorry," he said.

Quickly grabbed his falling hand, Amara tightened her grip. "I don't mind," she replied.

The two exchanged a brief but innocent glance before looking out to the pond once again. Amara lingered slightly longer, her eyes shifting nervously. It was as if she wanted to say more but failed to find the words and the expressionless look on her face did little to help. A heartfelt exchange was new to her, a virgin experience that was exciting and fresh. She could feel something changing inside of her, a feeling in her chest that Amara could only describe as painful.

"...I don't remember her; my mother," Amara said quietly, as if she only meant it for her ears alone. "I remember parts, pieces, but I can't remember her face."

Through her cold and faceless expression, Emrys could see a single tear ball up and run down her flushed cheek. He knew that it was likely a side effect of her habitual cataloging. Some memories - the meaningful ones - they were meant to last, but personal memories took low precedence over military intelligence. For a Mencist like Amara, slowly losing the memory of her mother was part of the job; it was part of what made her one of the best at what she did.

They said nothing for some time, and listened to the echoes of dripping water that fell from the ceiling, onto the pond below. Squeezing her hand gently, Emrys had no words to comfort her but he wanted to let her know that he was there. She eventually gave a subtle squeeze in return, letting him know that she was okay.

"There is another reason why I brought you here," Emrys said. "I am going to enlist with the UMI..." His words seemed to echo through the vast empty space and in the silence that followed.

Emrys held her hand more tightly before continuing. "My mother is dead today because of the UMI. They told my father that there was a better life here and he believed them. They told him so many things that turned out to be a complete farce, including the safety of this planet. Serec, especially Harvest, was infested with parasitic spores... She... My mother did not go peacefully... They claimed that the parasites arrived later, on the backs of a meteor shower."

"Was that much true?" Amara asked.

"I don't know. But after all of the other lies, I don't see why they would tell me the truth. That truth seemed too convenient," replied Emrys. He could not trust them, not after what they had done. For Emrys, the UMI was the closest incarnation of evil that he had known. Like his father had once told him, the UMI has taken everything.

"If you hold such a grudge against the UMI then why would you enlist?" Amara asked. It was a logical question. Everything that he had just explained seemed like a perfect excuse to stay as far from them as possible.

Emrys would not say, not exactly. At first he was quiet but Amara continued to press him. He could not tell her that he was going to join the UMI for her, that he wanted to earn the right to be with her. He could not say that he felt like he was beneath her, so he told her the only truth that he could say.

"I can't do this forever," Emrys said as he gestured to the caves around them. "The UMI is draining this site dry and leaving us with enough to live on, but never enough to break free. We came to Serec to get away from the settler's cycle."

"...Settler's cycle?" Amara asked.

"It means living from hand to mouth, under the thumb of the UMI. They have a talent for keeping their leashes tight and I don't suspect Harvest can resist much longer."

"So if you can't beat them, join them. Is that your grand strategy," she asked with a hint of sarcasm.

Amara was almost upset with his defense. She knew that he was angry at them, but it sounded like pure insanity to accept defeat. It took some time but Amara realized that she was more upset at the thought that he may not be on Serec very soon.

"Is that your only reason," she continued. "I wish that I had words to explain what the *Dogs of the Military* are forced to do. You enlist because you believe in the UMI or because you have no choice, those are the sane options..."

"...I have no choice," replied Emrys in a slightly raised voice. He promptly lowered his voice and continued, "There is something that your dad said to me; there is something that I need to do." He could not say anymore than that. Feeling like he had said too much already, Emrys turned away as if to avoid further discussion.

He knew Amara would call him a fool for enlisting, especially for the reasons that he could not say. Amara had lived her life, a very fine life, under the wing of a well decorated soldier. That kind of life had certain luxuries that Emrys could not provide, not as a miner's son. Emrys came from nothing, and was determined to reach greatness. He knew that it was stupid boyish pride but it was enough to break the settler's cycle, the cycle that he feared so much. His dreams were bigger than himself and he needed the power and wealth provided by the UMI to reach that status.

"I heard that there was a temporary base near the space port. I am going to take the placement exam tomorrow and they may want me to depart as early as that day." Emrys was growing tired. His mind was spinning with everything that had to be done. "We should head back, it's getting late."

They quickly worked their way out of the cave and back onto the tram. Looking up at the dimming sky, the day had passed by much quicker than he anticipated. The sun was encroaching on the twilight hours and the skies had already begun to change in color. Emrys was normally very good at judging his time underground, but being there with Amara and holding her hand caused him to lose track.

Thinking back to their conversion, Amara was shocked that he could be leaving Serec so soon. As they reached the tram stop in Harvest, Amara said, "We've only just met."

"I've known you my whole life, Amara; here and on Earth. I would not easily forget you," replied Emrys.

They both stepped down from the tram, Amara first followed by Emrys. Just as he took his final step down from the tram, Amara spun around and kissed him, gently on the lips. Her lips... Her lips felt like nothing else and he was lost in them, even if the kiss lasted for only a brief moment. As she pulled away slowly, he curled his lips in to savor the moment, to remember the taste of her lips.

"What... why...," asked Emrys who was still searching for the right words to say.

"I wanted to thank you for being a friend to me," she replied. Amara's reply was once again flat in tone but Emrys could not concentrate enough to sense her true feelings. Still, she appeared unshaken and composed. "Was it wrong of me to..."

"...No!" he exclaimed, "It was very right. It's just that... You don't go around kissing friends on the mouth like that do you?" he asked sheepishly.

"I... I've never had a friend," she calmly replied.

Emrys understood what she meant. He knew what life as a Mencist was like. A meaningful friendship was not something they taught at the academy. Still a bit shaken by the kiss, he was speechless for a moment, but managed to build the strength in his lips to smile.

"Why do you always smile like that? It's not the way you smile at anyone else," she said in a curious tone. "It's almost like you are in pain or something."

Emrys only smiled again, but this time more warmly. "Remind me to tell you some day," he replied.

"Is that a promise?" asked Amara in a serious and almost mechanical way.

Emrys was half expecting her to write a contract over their agreement. He chuckled at how serious she was over every detail in life. Eventually he nodded and watched as she turned and walked away. He did not move, not until she was clear out of sight. The thought of her kiss still tingled on his lips and painted a smile that was ear to ear. His once tired mind was now replaced with restless thoughts. It was going to be a long and sleepless night.

Chapter 15

Sitting across from Emrys was a portly man with sandy blonde hair and dark eyes. Judging from the uniform and the insignia that we wore, Emry could see that the man was the recruiting officer on duty. They sat together in a room that had little more than a metal table and two chairs that faced each other. It looked to be more like an interrogation chamber than a room to interview military candidates. On one wall was a large mirrored panel that Emrys could only assume was a one-way glass. Above them was an array of LED lights that colored the room in a cold and subtle aqua blue. Even the air in the room gave Emrys a chill; it was calm and almost damp on his skin.

The recruiting officer coughed a few times and continued to parse through the lines of scores that he had brought up on the tablet in front of him. Even his light coughing echoed against the hard metallic walls and every reverberant sound made the room appear larger than it really was. The lights flickered slightly, just enough for them both to take notice.

"Sorry about that," the recruiter said as he pointed carelessly up to the lights. "We are using poor power sources right now. Once the permanent base is constructed, we can get some steady power in here."

Emrys only nodded in response. He did his best to mask the smile that snuck onto his face. Harvest had converted to clean energy long ago. Serec's sun and wind were powerful enough to keep some of their largest cities in working order, with reserves. The UMI still relied heavily on toxic energy sources that were less reliable for long term use. They were likely powering the base directly from one of their ship's reactors; a classic hack job in his opinion.

"I have to be straight with you, I am a little confused," the recruiter noted. He was reading the scores for the placement test that Emrys had recently completed. "You scored nearly perfect on the exam, flawless intelligence scores, but you nearly failed social etiquette."

"That is a good thing right?" Emrys interrupted in a naïve and cheerful tone. The recruiter only looked at him like he was not from this world. It was not exactly the response that Emrys was expecting.

"I did a little digging," the recruiter continued. "It was not easy to find your academy papers. It says here that you graduated early, Valedictorian, from the Harvest Mencist Academy. A transfer student from the Mencist Academy in..."

"...I would appreciate it if those documents were kept classified," Emrys interrupted. His once cheerful tone was suddenly more shaken and unsettled.

Emrys' posture suddenly changed, and his calm demeanor melted away to reveal a much more agitated person inside. It was as if he did not expect the recruiter to find his records or to search as hard as he did. Hoping that the recruiter would have simply ignored his records after a surface level search had failed, Emrys underestimated his motivation.

The recruiter continued to look at Emrys curiously. "What are trying to hide," he asked.

"Becoming a Mencist was not my calling, and I would rather not have my education determine my future," Emry replied in a tone that was almost rehearsed. This was not the first time that Emrys had to defend his position, defend his right for the freedom to choose his own path, and he was confident that it would not be the last.

"Well, academy records or not, I can't place you as an enlisted soldier. There would be questions around that recommendation and, frankly kid, I am not going to lose my pension for you. I would have to give you an officer's recommendation. That is the best that I can do," the recruiter stated firmly.

That recommendation was good enough for Emrys. Though a Mencist was typically an advisory position, they were never far from the highest ranks. A standard officer's rank was below Emry's scores but it was better than becoming something that he would rather not be.

"Okay, I understand…" Emrys replied, but was quickly interrupted.

"I am done yet; there is more to this contract. We are looking for officer's to participate in a new program that the UMI is calling Project Dust. Heck, we might even be able to do something about that arm." The recruiter gestured to the scars that wrapped around Emry's forearm.

"I don't care about the scars but I wouldn't mind getting full mobility back," Emrys replied.

A wiry grin appeared on the recruiters face. "So, do we have a deal?" he asked.

Emry nodded in response and they both shook hands to finalize their agreement. Content over the agreement, the recruiting officer immediately began typing away on his tablet.

In a few short minutes the recruiter was done. Emrys was officially enlisted with a recommendation for a Warrant Officer's rank and an amendment into the Project Dust program. Looking at the current military bodies on Serec, both recommendations would likely be accepted without much resistance.

Compared to any militarized city on Earth, there was a noticeable lack of personnel in Harvest and even less of them were likely to accept experimental treatments. Emrys was not thrilled over the idea of applying for an ambiguous experiment but it was the only way to avoid the lifeless career of a Mencist. For some, like Amara, it may have been their greatest calling. But for someone like Emrys, the life of a Mencist was a death sentence.

It did not take a genius to know what kind of program Project Dust would be. The UMI was never very original and Emrys only knew because he was aware of the existence of Dust. It was a bit of knowledge that only the Harvest miners were aware of.

"My part is done. The Chief Researcher will be with you shortly," the recruiter gestured to someone who must have been waiting behind the glass. "...and brief you on the details of Project Dust. Good luck kid. Maybe next time we meet, I will be saluting you." The recruiter's words were empty. It was clearly a rehearsed phrase that he used to give nervous hopefuls a brief moment of confidence. Though his words lacked emotion, it did not make them any less true.

As a Warrant Officer, Emrys had surpassed what many would hope to achieve in their careers. The UMI did not move slowly, not when it came to recruiting. For all of the inefficiencies within their massive hierarchy, the process of enlisting soldiers was automated down to a science. It was nearly as easy as flipping a switch for anyone to be converted from civilian to enlisted status. Undoing that switch was. ...A little more difficult.

As the recruiting officer opened the door, he stepped back and made way for an elder woman who entered the room. The officer stood stiff, nearly at attention, and continued to face forward until the elder woman gestured for him to leave with a slight nod to the door. After a brief salute, the recruiting officer quickly stepped out and closed the door behind him. Judging from the officer's sudden change in behavior, Emrys concluded that this woman must have been someone of great importance.

Emrys studied the seemingly fragile old woman who wobbled her way to the chair that was once occupied by the recruiting officer. She wore dark, nearly opaque glasses that shrouded her eyes, and a white formal suit that was typical of medical personnel. The woman's silver hair was short but nearly blended with the color of her suit, and a scarce number of black stripes on her uniform helped to complete the patterns.

Staring at her with a puzzled look on his face, Emrys struggled to place her, to put a name to her face. The woman looked familiar; he must have seen her around Harvest for several years and not known who she was. He leaned in closer to the elder woman who sat nearly motionless and waved his hand across her face. She did not move; she did not flinch.

"I assure you that I am blind, but it does not mean that I cannot see." The woman spoke in a commanding voice. Her accent was enough to peak his interests.

Despite the woman's attempts to mask her voice, Emrys had never heard the accent of a descendent of the rebellion, but it was obvious to him. The rebellion had all but been abolished, and the only remnant of their existence was a language that few could understand. Part of the unification on Earth brought on by the UMI was a unified language, a mixture of the dominant societies of the time. As a form of language encryption, the rebels spoke in a lost tongue. Generations later, their splintered language has colored their accents, though few might have noticed the subtle trill in her voice. This woman was the product of a thousand years of revolt against the UMI. Somehow, they managed to escape the UMI for countless generations. Sitting back with curious grin on his face,

Emrys was intrigued to find one of them within the UMI's ranks.

"I did not expect, in all my years, to meet one of you," Emrys stated. He could see the elder woman's brows rise behind the opaque lenses on her face.

"And you continue to impress me Mr. Hughend. I don't think it needs to be said, but I have my reasons for being here just as you have yours. Let us leave it at that," she insisted.

It was clear that this woman could have him killed with the nod of her head. No one would even know that he was gone. She was a powerful figure, someone who commanded respect, someone that Emrys would be best to leave to her own devices. He politely nodded and never dared to mention it again.

"Tell me what you know about Dust, Mr. Hughend." The elder woman eased back as well as she could in the hard metallic chairs.

"Not much. As a miner's son, I know what to look for. It is a white crystallized mineral that is, in its raw form, mostly harmless and salty to the taste. Some of our crew had experienced severe cramps, headaches, and a few bloody noses but nothing fatal so far." Emrys continued to list a number of surface deep answers. He did his best to mask his suspicions of what Dust was being using for but the elder woman was not fooled.

"I thought we were past all of these games," she insisted.

"You asked me what I knew, not what I suspected," Emrys clarified. He twitched slightly when the woman chucked at his clarification. He could not explain the feeling but this woman made him uneasy, jumpy at best.

"I would expect no less from a Mencist, or is Warrant Officer? These recommendations do get mixed up all the time," the elder woman reminded Emrys of his fragile situation. She did not appreciate Emrys holding back his predictions, that much was clear to him now.

"I suspect that there is some form of super soldier experiments using Dust as the catalyst. I cannot imagine the UMI investing so much into something unless it was in preparation of a military arms race. Who is the enemy," Emrys asked.

"That is not your concern at this time," the woman responded.

From the uncertain turn of her head, Emrys could see that even she did not have all the answers to that question. In many ways, this menacing and powerful woman was just another link in the long chain of command. Whoever the new threat was, it must have shaken the UMI's confidence.

"Please continue," she asked from him.

"Given that large quantities of the raw mineral seem to inflict some form of physiological change, I can only guess that a pharmaceutical grade is being developed. But I have only seen people get sick from Dust."

"...Sick yes, but only from the poisonous compounds," the woman replied. "Dust, in raw form, is actually a toxic chemical compound found naturally on Serec. When broken into its parts, it can produce some very interesting results, results that we cannot synthesize for some reason."

"Are you telling me that we have been mining in poison shafts?" Emry snapped.

Brooding with disgust, he could only think of the many people sent home, sick from Dust poisoning. The image of his father, smiling, bathed in finely ground mineral on the day that they discovered the Dust deposits had changed for him now. All he could see now was his father, covered in poison, and his health being eaten away like the parasitic spores that killed his mother.

"Many of them have worked in those mines for over a decade and have survived. The poisonous compounds are not lethal if treated with rest and hydration," the woman calmly prescribed.

From her careless diagnosis, it was obvious that the woman viewed them all as test subjects. Emrys made the smart decision, not to argue any further. He was now a link in the military chain, and the UMI expressed zero tolerance for insubordinate behavior.

"I can assure you what once the compound has awakened in you that it will feel like nothing you have felt before," the woman insisted. "This particular compound is my best experiment yet. It is the first time that we've been able to fuse it with samples of DNA found within Sigil. You would be amazed at how quickly they bond to those cells, exponentially faster than human cells."

The brightened expression on the woman's face told Emrys that she must have taken the experiment herself. It would have explained her sixth sense about the movements and gestures around her, despite her diminished ocular ability. Emrys was beginning to see what Dust was capable of achieving. If it was true, this kind of power seemed unnatural and surreal.

"Consider yourself to be one of the Rector's first born, a child spawned from its divine DNA." The woman spoke in circle, ranting about the greatness of this newly created human race. "Welcome to the next generation of humankind," she uttered, leaning over the table and staring through Emrys with her cold white eyes.

"What about the others? How many people have you experimented on? What happened to them?" Emrys blurted out questions, giving no time for any of them to be answered.

"If you would please raise your sleeve," the woman insisted, ignoring his barrage of questions.

Emrys perked up, he had not anticipated that they would administer any drugs so quickly. "Hold on," he insisted as he witnessed two burly soldiers barge into the room.

The each of the men held one of Emrys' arms. The first man twisted his right arm behind his back and pushed his head down onto the table. Restraining Emrys with his weight, the second man laid Emry's left arm across the table and pinned it such that he could not move. With a look of wonderment painted across her face, the elder woman pulled out a needle that Emrys could only assume was the Dust compound.

"You strike me as a forward person, Mr. Hughend. I can probably attribute that to your academy training. So, let me be perfectly clear when I tell you that this... will... hurt..." With those final words, she stuck the needle into his arm and slowly injected the compound into his body.

Emrys could feel the thick compound pressing through his veins and his heart accelerating to keep up with the toxins that now ran through his body. Unable to concentrate from the noise that rattled in his head, Emry gripped at his scalp and pressed down to quiet reverberating ringing but it did not help. His blood was on fire as the tingling sensation grew from the injection point until his entire body was numb from the pain. In the moment that the two men had let go, Emrys fell to the floor, and like a lifeless body, hit the ground with a thud. As if someone had run a thousand volts through him, Emrys began to convulse uncontrollably. Struggling to regain control, he slowed his heart rate, but the stress was too much. After a brief and futile struggle against the toxic compound, Emrys felt his consciousness fade and the darkness take him.

Chapter 16

Without warning, Amara barged into the house and searched for her father. She did not have to search very long. Miles was having dinner with two other officials in the dining room, just across from the Den.

"How could you?" she yelled passionately.

"...Amara?" Miles questioned her in a surprised tone.

Stunned by her emotional instability, it was the first time he had ever seen her so unglued. His usually calm and calculated daughter had suddenly become a rambling emotional person. Standing over him but out of arms' reach, Amara paced back and forth across the threshold that separated the dining room from the main foyer. She was visibly irritated and Mile remained silent, waiting for her to explain this behavior.

"How could you do that to him? What did you say to him?" Each word from her mouth seemed to grow with frustration.

Amara grew more irate with time, knowing that her father must have done something to Emrys, he must have said something to push Emrys over the edge. She knew what kind of person Miles could be, and how easily he manipulated people.

"Oh, that young man Emrys? He is a grown up Amara and so are you, now start acting like one," his words spit fire but Miles did not bother to lift his head from the meal in front of him.

Miles took another bite of the savory dish, then a long sip of the coffee that was held in his hand. Waiting for Amara to walk away, Miles refused to acknowledge her as if to let her know that this conversation was over. He waited, but she did leave. Putting down his warm cup, Mile closed his eyes and clenched down on the fork that was still in his hand. Taking a deep breath, Miles put down his fork gently and turned to Amara to see a misty-eyed young woman standing across from him.

"...he was my friend," she snarled each word with unrestrained distain. "...he was my friend... You can't even imagine what that means."

Miles was clearly upset and embarrassed by her outbursts. He didn't understand; how could he? As a man of action, Miles was not a Mencist, nor did he take interest in her education. He knew that a life as a Mencist would ensure a fruitful future with the UMI. Conscious or not, Miles made a tactical decision for her many years ago, a decision that implied success was more important than happiness. He was a loving father but a lifelong career in the UMI left him with little time to learn how to raise a daughter. He could never understand what it meant for a Mencist to have a friend.

The two officials remained silent, in shock from the outrage being exhumed by a Mencist. It was something that they had never seen before, certainly not from a Mencist who had been trained by the finest academies on Earth. The culture on Serec, in Harvest was beginning to eat away at her armor plated heart; even Amara could sense that much in her fit of rage. She was becoming. ...Human.

"If he dies..." Amara paused for a moment to choke back the tears of frustration that threatened to come out. "If he dies, I will never forgive you." Quickly stormed out of the dining room, Amara left before her emotions overwhelmed her. Anymore words would have been pointless, and would have only served to enrage her even more.

After Amara stormed out, the meeting continued. "I apologizing gentlemen. They can be a bit unstable at this age." Miles watched as the two officials eased back into their chairs and chuckled. "She acts more like her mother every day," he said in a much calmer voice. His words were more heartfelt than before and he appeared to be reminiscing on the past for a brief moment.

As she stormed out of the room, Amara turned back on last time. She heard the Colonels comment and rebutted with a scornful glare. Catching a glance of his dazed appearance, she would have felt sorry for him if she wasn't so angry at the time. Amara knew that he still loved them both, her and her mother. But even love and affection was never enough to hold together the bonds that tied them, she learned that long ago.

"Now," Miles continued, "It looks like we will be mobilizing sooner than expected. As the highest ranked officer on location, until the fleet arrives I'll be the acting General. We may only have enough troops for Black ops reconnaissance..." His words seemed to fade into nothingness as they became more and more secretive.

...Military strategies? Amara was confused; why were they having strategic meetings on a small settlement town? Finally, with his words down to a whisper, Amara could no longer hear the mumbling sounds. She waited just around the corner to listen more closely but their voices were lost. Peeking around the corner, Amara could only read one word from his lips, "...invasion".

Chapter 17

At first, Emrys could see nothing but darkness. It took some time for him to realize that his eyes were closed. He was so disoriented that he could not tell up from down or if he was awake or dreaming. Eventually, he did open his eyes but his vision was consumed with a flash of white. The bright lights and white walls of the sickbay seemed to blur together. It took a minute for his eyes to adjust, but when they did it was an even greater shock.

Emrys was shackled to a bed and connected to an array of medical devices. He could see through the backs of the many glass displays that they were monitoring his every condition. Still attempting to steady his mind, Emrys could sense that they must have used some form of accelerant. His heart was racing and his anxiety was higher than he had ever felt before. With his lungs pulsing violently, Emrys felt his like he was breathing at a far accelerated rate.

"Professor, he is coming to," a voice calmly stated.

Emry focused on the moving bodies that shuffled around him as they continued to poke and prod at the various devices nearby. The voice came from a medical staff member who was standing to his left. At the foot of the bed was a figure far more familiar to him, the elder woman. She must have been this professor person, it was the only conclusion that Emrys could piece together in his clouded mind.

"How are you feeling?" the elder woman asked in a polite voice. Her soothing kindness irritated Emrys like nothing else.

"Crazy old hag," every word scratched at his throat. Now feeling the grit in the back of his throat, Emrys had barely noticed his chapped lips and dry mouth until now. "You stuck me we some kind of poison. How do you think I am feeling?"

"I apologize," she said, though her words were flat and heartless. "Adrenaline is the trigger to awaken the compound and drastic measures must be taken sometimes. Have you awakened yet?"

"I am speaking to you am I not," he retorted.

"Mr Hughend, let us not start these games again. I wish to know if you have awakened."

"I don't feel any different," he replied in a spiteful tone.

"That is a shame," she mumbled. The professor reached for a display that rested at the foot of the bed. Swiping through the medical logs line by line, she made a few inaudible sounds as she read through each one. "Your constitution is strong, I will give you that much. I gather that you must have calmed your nerves before passing out. Even the adrenaline shots we've been administering regularly don't seem to be reacting."

"If you are trying to kill me, a gun might be more effective," Emrys snorted in a sarcastic tone.

The professor ignored his snarky comment and continued to analyze the next stage in his treatments. "I will have the acting General assign you to one of the reconnaissance teams who are heading out soon. Perhaps a little time in the field will elevate your levels."

Emrys wanted to reply but his strength was fading and his mind continued to spin and swell with thoughts. With his consciousness fading in and out for what felt like an eternity, he had visions of his childhood and dreams that felt so surreal that he didn't know if they were his own. The concoction of chemicals running through his body left him in an endless cycle of pain and bliss; in the fine line between sleep and awake.

An unknown amount of time had passed for Emrys, but he eventually regained his strength and the medications had finally stopped. In his brief moments of clarity, Emrys heard many rumors that circulated the halls of the sickbay. The only rumor to strike a tone with him was the one about the acting General, a man named Colonel Miles Binson.

"I just had to see this for myself," a familiar voice called out. In an almost twisted fate, Miles stepped into the room. It was as if Emrys had inadvertently called for him through his thoughts. "So, you are trying to be someone I see," Miles remarked in casual tone.

"Something like that," replied Emrys. He kept his voice low and polite but the tension between them was clear from the moment he stepped into the room.

"I must say, I like that fire about you. You are fighter, like your old man. You don't take shit from anyone," exclaimed Miles with a wide smile.

Miles appeared more impressed by Emrys' brooding anger than his sense of pride. It was clear to Emrys that the Colonel was a man of action, a man who saw more value in the fight than the outcome. A sudden gesture, like a suicidal experience for the greater good of the UMI, struck a chord for Miles. Though it was not entirely voluntary, Emrys would take the praise any way he could; after all, Miles was his catalyst for enlisting.

With that grin still on his face, Miles continued. "That is why I chose your dad to come and form Harvest, to mine that site. A fighter never quits; he always finds a way. Do you understand?" Miles asked.

Emrys wasn't exactly certain of what Miles was trying to say. Instead of asking for clarification, he simply nodded. Perhaps Miles suddenly had a new found respect for Emrys. *Was it that easy?* He asked himself. He wondered if the line between the classes of citizen and soldier were in fact so wide for a man like Miles. Emrys found it to be a strange distinction to make but he had not yet experienced life on the front lines. Maybe there was something to the brotherhood that Miles instantly could relate to.

"Warrant Officer Hughend, now that is a surprise," said Miles. "I am even more surprised that you would agree to this program after what you have seen at the dig site," implying the streak of illnesses surrounding the Dust mines.

Emrys was afraid to admit that he had not seen the signs. The illnesses were not common enough to raise any red flags and only occurred in the rare times when a deposit of Dust was found. He closed his eyes for a brief moment. It pained him not to know how his father and the crew were doing after the last deposit. It was the largest deposit of mineral that they had seen in all of their years. It might have been enough to kill them all.

"I can see from the look on your face that you are worried," insisted Miles. "I assure you that you will live through this." Emrys slowly shook his head with his eyes still closed. "Ah, your father?" Miles asked. Emrys nodded and finally opened his eyes eagerly. "Everyone is being properly treated before the signs appear. It would be a nightmare if we had to staff up at a time when we needed them most."

Emrys was disgusted by his reasoning but the logic made perfect sense to him. The UMI did not want to deal with the manual efforts of colonizing a town that had been destroyed by Dust. Rebuilding the mining operations would have been an expensive endeavor. The Council would have severely disciplined anyone involved, including the Colonel himself. Though Miles did not clarify, Emrys could only assume that they were not told of the toxins in Dust. The treatments were probably being masked as some form of immunization protocol.

Miles looked at an empty chair that rested in the corner of the room. He wheeled the chair next to the bed and sat down. Sitting erect in the chair, Miles crossed his arms and began to dictate his reason for the unexpected visit.

"Let me brief you on why I am here," stated Miles. It seemed that he was done with the pleasantries and quickly shifted back to the stone faced man that Emrys first met. "We have been planning a reconnaissance mission for a nearby planet called Seizonrenda. There were a number of small colonies on the planet but intelligence tells us that they may be in trouble. I'm told that all colonies have had radio silence for nearly six weeks now."

"...Intelligence?" Emrys asked.

"This one is above my pay grade." Miles replied with absolute honesty. The expression on his face told Emrys that he was as curious as anyone.

As any good soldier would do, when orders come down from the top, it was their job to follow them. Emrys could see that this was no different than any other mission for Miles, an age old tradition to receive intelligences on a need-to-know basis.

"What are we looking for?" Emrys asked.

"We are looking for anything you can find. We're not sure what has caused the radio silence but we're hoping that it has something to do with the storm patterns we are seeing from orbit. I'll be going on this mission as the acting General and waiting for your report from orbit."

"Who else is going down there with me?" Emrys asked with widened eyes. It seemed like he had nothing but questions but he wanted to be as prepared as possible.

"You will be a part of a small team. Your job, Warrant Officer, is to observe and report. Their job is to make sure that you come back alive. It is one of the perks of being a ranked officer." Miles was almost smug with his words.

Emrys couldn't help but to keep wondering why Miles had a change of heart with him. Maybe part of his new found respect had less to do with him enlisting and more to do with the rank that he had achieved. It was something that Emrys might never quite grasp.

"Get some sleep," Miles quietly uttered. "We leave in less than 48 hours."

Chapter 18

From an open window, a clove-like scent blew into Amara's bedroom. A low bench that usually sat at the foot of her bed was pressed against the window now, and she sat there peacefully enjoying the fresh Harvest air. It was a strange feeling for her to accept still, the thought of unfiltered air filling her lungs freely or the clear breeze in her hair. Even the sun was warm on her face, much different from the holographic displays that plastered Earth. The faint glow of those artificial rays did not compare to the tingling sensation she now felt on her skin, a feeling that she could only describe as powerful.

The gardens in Harvest were scarce but very real, and tickled her senses. She made just the slightest of twitches at the edge of her mouth. One might have almost mistaken it for a smile, but they were gone more quickly than they appeared. Amara was happy on Harvest and she was happy to wait for her friend to return safely.

Life was beginning to make sense here in her new home, and she could feel the faintest of flames in her heart. It was a feeling that she could not describe; how could she? It was the first time that she met someone who understood her plight. It was the first time that someone like Emrys accepted her as something more than a living computer, he saw the human inside of her.

Her near smiles that faded in and out were not unprovoked however. She had been listening to Emrys' voice, by way of a data log. Transmitted to her personal tablet, the audio log continued to play and provoke more from Amara.

> *Audio Log – ehughend.001*
>
> *I am sorry that I can only send audio logs. For security reasons, I am not able to... I am sure that you know the drill, with your dad being gone on tours all the time.*
>
> *This is my first transmission as a UMI officer and it feels a bit strange. I would have never thought to find myself on a tour of duty for the UMI. This is (laughs)... It is hard to believe. I am not exactly sure what I wanted to say; I never know what to say to these things. The professor has insisted that I record these logs so they can track my mental stability or something. I figured if I was going to record myself saying something that I should be saying those things to someone, right?*
>
> *Well, I guess I just wanted to say... I hope you are doing well on Harvest. I will do my best to keep him safe; you know who (laughs). I am sure that he will probably be doing the safe keeping. I can't really say more than that. Just know that we should all be home in four to six weeks. You'll barely know that we were gone.*
>
> *Okay... This is Warrant Officer Emrys Hughend, signing out.*

Amara knew exactly who Emrys was talking about. Miles had said very little to Amara before leaving on this mission, he didn't even tell her that Emrys would be going as well. Miles rarely ever said much to her just before a mission and she never knew why. She only speculated that he had to change his state of mind from a family man to a man of honor.

Many years have passed since Amara was old enough to truly know what her father did and the routine was always the same. Miles never talked before his missions and her spat with him just days before his departure did not help to smooth things over. It was no surprise that Amara had to discover the whereabouts of Emrys through an audio log that he transmitted to her. She took some comfort in knowing that they were together. Emrys was clumsy and helpless but Amara felt more at ease in knowing that he was under her father's command.

Amara continued to sit next to her bedroom window, long after the recording had stopped. It was quickly becoming her favorite place to sit whenever she was home alone. Her bedroom was easily the most decorative room in the house and her window faced the late evening sun. The muted sky that once kept Amara up to all hours of the night was a welcome sight to her now. Emrys had shown her the sun, setting beneath the white dunes and now she craved it nearly every night. Serec was beginning to feel like home, more than her life on Earth ever felt.

Not a word was whispered or a noise was made in the last minutes just before twilight. Amara shared a moment of silence and hoped that her friend was out there somewhere, sharing it with her. Wishing him the best and hoping for a safe return was the closest thing to praying that she had ever known. *It would have to do,* she thought.

After one last deep breath of the scented air that blew past her window, the bed was calling her name. Tomorrow would be an important day for Amara as well. With formal training behind her, it would be her first day at the academy, as a full member of the staff. She gently slipped under her tightly fitted sheets and nuzzled into her bed until it felt right.

Turning her head to face the window, Amara could see one faint glimmer in the sky. It could have been a star, a rare find for the muted night sky. But she knew in her heart that it must have been Emrys and Miles, wishing her one last goodnight before leaving orbit.

Chapter 19

Only a faint light from the projected image on the wall could be seen in the darkened room filled with soldiers. Emrys and other soldiers who were tasked to obtain information from the surface of Seizonrenda were gathered in the room for briefing. Colonel Miles was going on about their mission but Emrys was too lost in his own thoughts.

Questioning if he had made the right choice, Emrys recounted the few small steps that he had taken and how far it had already brought him. In a matter of weeks, he had found himself on the frontlines of a potentially dangerous confrontation with an unknown force. This was not at all what he had anticipated and Emrys was beginning to feel the ramifications of his naivety. He could do nothing but sit a listen to the final words that Miles had to offer.

"...And let me say this just once more. You are not to engage with the locals or otherwise down there, not unless explicit permission is given by Orbital Command." Miles reiterated his warnings.

Colonel Miles continued to drill into their minds that this was to be a reconnaissance mission and nothing more. As Emrys look around the room, he saw a collection of grizzled and war hardened men and women. Emrys thought that perhaps the fears that Miles shared may have been justified, and his warnings had to be made clear.

As he continued to watch the soldiers in the room more than the Colonel, Emrys peeled away at their physiological conditions. His Mencist training was rusty, but nearly two decades of reprogramming was a hard habit to break. The subtle smirks under their skin, the snorts and whispers under their breath; it would be a concern for any officer in command to leave these war fighters alone.

The rebels were a small but constant threat for the UMI and these soldiers had seen their share of human resistance. For Emrys, he had no doubt in his mind that every soldier here was prepared to neutralize any rebel insurgents who dared to show their face. A complete radio silence could only mean one thing, a resistance group had risen and a coordinated strike was issued to all UMI colonies on Seizonrenda. Emrys was impressed that the rebels could coordinate such an attack, but he had his suspicions. A unified radio silence on a planet-wide scale would involve a massive force, one that seemed greater than any insurgency; maybe even greater than the UMI.

"...Dismissed," Miles called out, and everyone scattered to their respective stations.

"Warrant Officer Hughend," a firm voice called out, "My name is Sergeant Clark, and I will be the point leading on our mission. Please come with me." Every word was professional and Sergeant Clark barely skipped a beat in his protocol. He greeted Emrys as a Sergeant should greet a superior officer.

Emrys felt a bit strange, seeing that he was much younger than the Sergeant who had salt and pepper sprouts of hair that were cut short on nearly all sides. The Sergeant was a tall man with a sturdy frame and a seriousness that Emrys found hard to ignore.

Emrys continued to follow Sergeant Clark down the twisted paths of the command ship until had they reached the launch bay. All the while, Emrys was being lectured

on the protocols of their mission. The Sergeant went into
shallow descriptions of their launch procedures and
continued to explain the dangers to look for once they
landed on the surface of the planet.

"I know that this is your first tour, and we will do
everything we can to make sure you get home in one
piece." Sergeant Clark's voice was firm, offering the only
words of hope that he could. It was suddenly clear to
Emrys that there were no promises in battle, only words
of hope.

The launch bay was a large circular chamber with
multiple dropships that stood upright against the hull.
Emrys watched as one of the dropships was launched
through the floor like a torpedo and his heart dropped.
The uttering sounds of an operator voice could be heard
in the background, calling out numbers and launch
patterns while groups of soldiers were running back and
forth and preparing for their drop. Some teams were
huddled in prayer while others simply waited in silence
for their turn.

In the center of the launch bay, a large table displayed
a holographic image of Seizonrenda and red orbital
markers littered the planet. He could only assume that
they were markers from other teams who had already gone
to investigate the planet surface as well. Watching the
glowing red markers that flickered like tiny angelic halos,
Emrys could see that this mission had turned out to be
much larger than he would have expected. The knots in
the pit of his stomach confirmed his suspicions that he
was not being told the whole truth.

"Holy shit Sarge, who is the jail bait," a woman with a
gruff tone stood eye to eye with Emrys.

The woman was about as tall as Emrys and shared a
build that was almost as muscular. The standard issue
UMI tank top made the definition of her arm muscles all
the more clear and her wavy jet black hair could have

easily fallen to her shoulders if it were not tied into a ponytail. She was obviously older than Emrys, but he could not tell exactly how old. Inspecting her from head to toe, Emrys could see that her face looked young but her demeanor said otherwise.

"That is Lance Corporal Mendoza," Sergeant Clark replied, "and that kid over there is Private Jenkins." Sergeant Clark pointed to the young man with short cherry blonde hair and fair skin.

The "kid" looked to be close to Emrys' age but he was much more restless than Emrys would have imagined from a war fighter. Pvt. Jenkins was a stringy young man who looked a bit out of place. Emrys speculated that Jenkins might have reconsidered enlisting if he had known that active tours were still part of the job. Outside of the small insurgencies that cropped up on occasion, the UMI had not seen a global threat in centuries so Emrys was not surprised to see at least one soldier who was never ready for the fight. In many ways, Emrys sympathized with Jenkins; he would have never imagined himself in this position either.

Emrys stood and watched as Pvt. Jenkins sat on a stack of crates and nervously loaded cartridges with full charge rounds. Upon further inspection, he could see the elongated casings and sharpened heads. Emrys was surprised to see high velocity rounds being loaded for what he thought would be a simple reconnaissance mission.

"Warrant Officer on deck, Lance Corporal," Sergeant Clark corrected Mendoza, and with that she stiffened up and offered a salute. Sergeant Clark then turned to Emrys and explained, "She has a foul mouth but Lance Corporal Mendoza is also one of the best Techs in the Corps; sorry about that Warrant Officer."

Emrys kindly answered the salute before saying, "At ease Lance Corporal. I have not earned that salute yet."

Emrys spoke without thinking and the strange look on her face told him that Mendoza did not understand.

Looking around the launch bay filled with war torn veterans, he did not feel entitled to the rank of an officer, not without a single day of active duty under his belt. Emrys was determined to achieve greatness and he kept Amara in his thoughts the entire time. As grand as it may have seemed, Emrys was content to earn his respect and the patch on his arm did little for him right now.

"...Sir?" asked LCpl Mendoza.

"Nevermind," Emrys mumbled as he gestured to Jenkins who was still loading full charge rounds. "High velocity rounds for a scouting mission; it seems a bit much, don't you think?" he asked kindly.

"Chance favors the prepared, Warrant Officer," Sergeant Clark replied. Emrys knew that he was paraphrasing an 18th century scientist. It was a phrase that was often repurposed for the early era of the UMI and became a form of mantra for the Corps.

"JQ0214, ready for orbital drop in T minus four minutes," the operator voice hailed through the data-link. Everyone in the team perked up and Emrys knew that their number was up.

The team filed into the dropship which was designed to launch four personnel at a time. The padded seats were nearly at a standing position but allowed each passenger their own seat and harness. Fashioned into a circular pattern around the inside of the empty vessel, each seat faced another as they were oriented into the four corners. Not noticing how nervous he really was, Emrys was barely able to lock himself into the multipoint harness.

His hands shook uncontrollably until Mendoza leaned in and steadied them. Holding his hands gently, she softly placed them on his lap and let her fingers graze his as she pulled away. She looked him straight in the eyes, almost seductively, and put her hand on his chest. Emrys' eyes widened slightly as he felt his legs pushing him harder into the seat to escape her hand that crept down his chest, toward his groin. He nervously winched, unsure of what she was doing but was quickly put at ease by the clicking sound of his harness that was then fasten into place. Tugging on the harness hard enough to make Emrys exhale, Mendoza gave him a hard slap on the shoulder to let him know that he was locked in tight.

Sitting back into her own chair, Mendoza shared a chuckle with the Sergeant who could only look away to keep from laughing out loud. Emrys could see that those two took some kind of pleasure in playing mind games with their green members. Watching the subtle expressions that they shared, it said a lot to Emrys. It told him that the Sargent and the Lance Corporal must have seen a lot of war time together. They barely said much to each other, but their visual language appeared to be more than enough to know what the other was thinking.

"Any tips for the way down," Emrys quivered out a few nervous words.

"Tips for the way down? Hell, it's only half as fun as the way up," LCpl Mendoza replied, "Then you'll get to see why they call this the Slingshot."

"Whatever you do, try not to pass out!" Sergeant Clark yelled out as the dropship began rattling and squealing like a turbine engine. "We lost a couple of guys last week; they passed out and never woke up."

Emrys' eyes widened as he concentrated on his breathing and rechecked his harness. He was so busy going through the flight check in his mind that he failed to notice the mischievous grin that Clark and Mendoza were sharing. Even Jenkins was suddenly too busy with his own flight checks to notice.

When his checks were done and his head was rested against the cushioned headrest, Emrys counted along with the launch sequence in his head. He started from ten and ran down the numbers along with the operator who was synchronized with all of their data-links. When the count reached one, Emrys could feel his stomach rise into his heart as the ship launched at a sudden breakneck speed.

The forces were incredible, more than Emrys had ever imagined and it was not long before he felt a dizziness coming over him. The sudden inebriated reaction that clouded his senses propelled a prickling sensation across his body, a sensation that seemed to linger on his skin and raise the hairs on his back. The rattling ship sounded like it was ready to tear open at the seams as Emrys listened to the crackling thud of atmospheric debris beating against the hull. He fought to keep his eyes open but the faint consciousness that remained was not enough to fight off the darkness.

Chapter 20

The uneasy rattling was enough to suddenly wake Emrys from his deep sleep. He woke to a snickering Pvt. Jenkins who was laughing at his expense. Tightening the strap on his rifle, Sergeant Clark barely noticed that Emrys had woken up and continued to ready his weapons.

"Okay, keep it down, you just woke up our resident officer," said Sergeant Clark. He did his best to remain professional but it was clear that he took some enjoyment from it as well. "It's okay Sir, it happens to a lot of first-timers."

Emrys looked around to collect himself and saw that he was strapped into a chair using a 5-point harness. The gentle rocking motion from inside of the cramped space told him that they must have been riding in some form of transport vehicle. Emrys speculated that it must have been dropped after the crew, or it was already on the ground waiting for them. Perpendicular to the motion of the vehicle , he sat in one of many chairs that were stacked next to each other; one row along the left side of the small enclosure and another row along the right. Both rows were facing each other and it left little more than a meter of leg room between the two.

Tapping his knuckle against the wall of the enclosure, Emrys could see that it was made of a dense metal. The reinforced metal walls affirmed his suspicion that they were riding in a military vehicle but not one that he had ever seen. Just over his head, a circular door appeared to grant access to the roof of the vehicle. Sergeant Clark noticed the puzzled look on his face but offered nothing to quell his curiosity.

"No windows..." mumble Emrys. He directed his comment openly, hoping that someone would answer him. For a short time no one did.

"Not much to look at out there," replied Sergeant Clark. After noticing that Jenkins was not responding, he continued to explain. "Whatever did this, they really worked this planet over. We've got reports from Orbital Command that our scout teams across the globe are seeing pretty much the same thing."

"We came, we saw; what the hell are we still doing here Sarge," Pvt. Jenkins asked as he was repeatedly cocking his weapon in a nervous fashion.

"First, steady that weapon Private before I steady it for you," warned Sergeant Clark with a firm look on his face. "Second, we are here to do our job. We observe and report until Orbital Command says we are done. We do not engage."

Emrys could see that everyone was on edge and the tension in the claustrophobic space was almost too much to contain. Whatever they saw; whatever was out there, it was enough to shake their resolve and that was enough to leave Emrys feeling helpless. He watched as each of the men checked and rechecked every coil and trigger on their gun. The directive was clearly not to engage but these men appeared to have other plans. Perhaps they were expecting the worse. Who could blame them when chance favors the prepared?

"Can I have my gun now," Emrys asked, "at least my sidearm?" Noticing that his sidearm was not holstered, he needed anything to make him feel more protected.

The Sergeant looked at Emrys' quivering eyes then glanced around to Jenkins who said nothing. They all quietly stared and waited for anyone to say anything as if there was something that no one wanted to reveal. Finally the Sergeant gave a quiet sigh before reaching behind his seat and pulling out a small caliber hand pistol. Pulling the clip and cocking the shaft, he ensured that no rounds were left in the barrel. The Sergeant then placed the clip back in and locked it into place with a tap of his palm.

The pistol was a standard issue sidearm for UMI soldiers in the field. Emrys had shot it many times before, throughout his academy training. Marksmanship was a requirement for graduation and though Emrys never scored the highest marks, he considered his own skills to be passable. The crystal charges and liquid oxygen primers made it one of the most deadly firearms in history and Emrys knew enough to respect that. Those chemical compounds in the casings were yet another militarized adaptation of research data found in the Sigil. Emrys wondered if the aliens had intended it to be used as a way to launch primitive projectiles, like the humans had done, or if the super heated chemical reaction could be used for something far more powerful.

"No disrespect Warrant Officer, but do me a favor and try not to shoot yourself in the foot," warned Sergeant Clark.

"None taken," replied Emrys.

Turning the gun around, he reached out to offer the weapon to Emrys who had already extended his hand. Before letting go of the pistol, Sergeant Clark reached with his other hand and turned on the weapons' safety device. He calmly let go of the sidearm and allowed Emrys to promptly holster it. The approving look on the Sergeants' face told Emrys that he had at least done that much right.

Before Emrys could say anymore, the vehicle had come to a complete stop and two strong knocks could be heard from the driver's compartment. At first Emrys struggled with his harness but was able to jar it loose. He followed behind each soldier who took their turn and filed out of the vehicle one at a time.

The transition from the darkened hollow of the vehicle to the blistering heat just outside was overwhelming and nearly took his breath away. Emrys slowed his breathing and took the dry air in through his nose and exhaled from his mouth. The musty smell that filled his lungs and tickled his nose forced Emrys to cough lightly, pushing out the burning stench. Holding his hand up to his face, Emrys made a futile attempt to mask the aroma of charred remains. The light from the flat but saturated sky was blinding at first and he questioned if his eyes would ever adjust.

"AR goggles up," barked Sergeant Clark. The men quickly shielded their eyes with shaded glasses that hugged the contours of their face.

Still blinded by the bright light, Emrys fumbled to find his goggles, but he soon found them dangling just underneath his neck and placed them over his eyes. Instantly the goggles monitored his retinal width and adjusted the darkness of the lenses accordingly. He could see clearly now and the Augmented Reality displays showed a myriad of information blitzing across his eyes as the goggles were constantly scanning anything and everything in his view. What Emrys saw then, he could not believe.

Standing near a cliff, Emrys peered over the massive ravine that must have been half of a kilometer deep. He could barely see the other side but it was enough to know that he was on the edge of a massive meteor crater. Focused on the enormous chasm just ahead, he failed to notice the rest of the terrain around him. There were more craters, many more. The ground was littered with impact debris, finally painting a picture for the air which smelled like sulfur and coal.

Upon closer inspection, Emrys could see a faint sheen that glistened from the soil beneath his feet. He tried to collect some of the soil but it was petrified, and only the soot that rested on top was easily smeared away. Like sheets of crystal amber and topaz, the sand had been melted into rocky shards of colored glass. He quickly came to realize that it was not only the soil beneath his feet; the glassy sheen persisted as far as he could see into the horizon.

Between the specks of shine, a dull shade of black ash rained down from the heavens like flakes of snow. The ash was piled high in some places, telling Emrys that it must have been falling for some time. It appeared to be an eternal downfall, a never ending flurry of onyx rain, a veritable Ashland.

"...what the hell," Emrys mumbled as he could only stare. His body failed to move any further from the shock of what he had seen. Emrys searched for them, but he had no words to describe what had happened. He had only heard of the rich vegetation and snow capped mountains of Seizonrenda, but all he could see was a barren land of craters and glass shards that jutted from the earth like crystal statues.

"Reentry temperatures of space projectiles can reach levels of over 1700 degrees Celsius. Larger mass means more velocity and a harder impact. Every one of these strikes was like setting off a few million tons of holy shit. Nothing ever had a chance down here," uttered LCpl Mendoza.

Her statement was enough to explain the cloud patterns that were detected from orbit. They were mistaken for storm systems, not fallout from a meteor strike. It could also explain why recon teams around the planet were having similar reports.

Emrys' mind was spinning from the overwhelming influx of information. The fallout, the similar reports around the globe, the inexplicable barrage of meteors, and the sudden radio silence from all of the colonies at once; they all seemed related and yet there was a missing link to bind them all together. The fact that there was any sunlight at all meant that the strike must have occurred a long time ago, possibly decades. He wanted to stop and process it all, but there was no time to think.

"Okay, listen up," said Sergeant Clark. "The day is still early but we have to go on foot from here. The sensors have detected movement about two klicks north from our position. We need to leave the rover here and proceed with caution..."

"...cloaks?" Pvt. Jenkins interrupted.

"Run your diagnostics now and keep them on standby. We can't waste the charge unless we have to," replied the Sergeant.

With those words, the team ran a diagnostics on their light-refracting ghillie cloaks to make sure they were in working order. Each soldier called out, "check". After another soldier circled around them to verify the cloak was functional then replied, "clear" and continued to the next soldier. Emrys did the same for his own suit, but he was hopeful that they would not need to use it.

Not long after their routine checks, the team set out to investigate the reading that was being displayed on their motion sensors. They continued to step lightly through the treacherous terrain and avoid serious injury from the glass shards that frosted the ground. On their way, Emrys took photos, both with his AR goggles and mental images to describe to Amara of what he had seen.

Scattered throughout the ragged terrain, the mixture of blacken dust that Emrys rubbed between his fingers seemed to be the only constant. It appeared to be ash from something organic that once lived there; perhaps the trees or shrubs, maybe human being... The soot that rained down continued to build up on their gear, and it quickly became a part of their routine to wipe clean the debris to ensure their devices were in working order.

At their pace it was only a few short minutes before they had reached the source of the blip on their sensors. Emrys and the others could see an almost human-like figure standing at the top of a ridge. With the rising sun to its back, even the AR goggles had trouble identifying who or what was standing there. It had not yet noticed them and Sergeant Clark motioned for everyone to get down. He then motioned for everyone to group up just behind a large barrier that occluded their view.

"Okay Mendonza, talk to me," whispered the Sergeant. His voice was steady and Emrys was more than impressed with the Sergeant's cool and calculating attitude.

"We've got two blips on that ridge, one must be on the other side," she replied. Mendoza struggled with her sensor for a bit, tapping furiously and questioning the results. Finally, she sighed and continued with the only information that the sensor was reporting. "Sarge... I don't think that blip is human..."

"What do you mean; like a bear or something?" Jenkins blurted with a tremble in his voice.

"No, not a fucking bear, Jenkins," Mendoza replied scornfully before turning her attention back to the Sergeant. "We may have contact with some full blown E.T. shit here Sarge. Nothing this big should have a heart rate that fast." She quietly peaked around the ashy boulder to allow her AR goggles to read its dimensions. "I'm guessing that it's resting idle right now, which means that it might be as tall as seven maybe seven and a half feet."

"Alright," Sergeant Clark sighed, "It's time to cloak up. We need to survey this thing and find out if we are dealing with a hostile alien race. Just in case, safeties off and make sure you have one in the barrel."

Without another words, the team suited up and checked their weapons. After enabling their cloaks, they each took turns inching up closer to the target. Tapping on the side of his AR goggles to magnify his view, Emrys squinted to better focus through the fog of black snow.

The figure slowly took shape as the sun rose higher and out from behind the shadowing silhouette. Emrys was shocked to see something that looked human in some ways but had almost insect-like features. The boney exoskeleton was only the beginning of its unique traits, and Emrys could see the eyes and mandible that were more resembling of a mantis than a human.

The alien lurched up, stretching its elongated arms after a long rest. It sent chills down Emrys' spine to think of those arms getting a hold of him and what they might do. He watched as the alien broke off a shard of glassed earth and began to chew it. It continued to break off various pieces as if it was looking for a distinct flavor in the rainbow of colored shards. Watching the creature grind shards between its mandibles, Emrys was suddenly overcome with curiosity.

"Holy shit Sarge, tell me you are seeing this," Mendoza commented. She used her data-link instead of verbal conversation. From this distance, it was hard to tell if the alien creature would be able to hear them speak.

Looking down at the ground below, Emrys was paralyzed with one thought; he had to confirm the hypothesis for himself. Still hidden by the cloak that was draped over him, Emrys used his field knife to quietly chip away a piece of the hardened soil. The ground was not glassy like he had seen before; something was different about this location. There was a reason why this creature was there and Emrys was determined to know why.   He placed the chip between the knife and a nearby stone, grinding it repeatedly until it was nothing more than a fine crystal powder. Placing a pinch of the grounded soil on his tongue, Emrys' suspicions and fears were confirmed all at once.

The unique taste was all he needed to know that there were traces of Dust in the ground. Seizonrenda's destruction and Dust were connected; these alien creatures were somehow creating this raw mineral. Until now, it was thought that Dust was unique to Harvest and something that could only be mined. If they were the creators of Dust then the Sigil may have been a ship left behind from their last visit to Harvest. Emrys concluded that if these creatures had suddenly returned to reap their creation, Harvest and all of Serec was in grave danger.

Just then, the second blip appeared from the other side of the ridge. It was some kind of beast that prowled around on four legs. Emrys thought that it could have been mistaken for some monstrous breed of dog but the snarling jaws and the boney plate that formed its face were like nothing he had ever seen. The hairless beast had skin that glistened like the scales of a snake, and it snorted violently like some kind of swine from hell.

A strange clicking noise could be heard from the first alien who was possibly the master of that beast. Emrys speculated that it must have been communicating with the beast through some common language. The alien turned its head toward the team and continued to stare in their direction suspiciously. Emrys could almost feel its eyes shooting through him.

"Can that thing see us?" asked Jenkins through his data-link.

"Not likely, we are cloaked," Sergeant Clark replied, "As long as you stop fidgeting we'll be fine."

"Then why the hell is that thing looking at us?" Jenkins uttered.

Even through the data-link, Emrys could sense that Jenkins' nerves were shot. The sight of an alien was enough to put him on edge, but the thought of it being hostile had clearly sent him over. Jenkins started inching back toward the boulder where they had originally grouped up. He had barely moved a few meters before his forearm caught a jagged edge of glass and sliced his arm deep. Biting down on his lip to dull the pain in his arm, Jenkins watched as the blood had begun to quickly pool underneath him. He said nothing to the others.

"Jenkins, I swear I will shoot you myself if you don't settle the fuck down," warned Mendoza.

Just then the beast raised its head and began snorting loudly once again. It paced from side to side and began to look irritated and excited. At first the beast slowly wandered in their direction but eventually sped up to a full gallop.

"What the hell just happened, Sarge. Why is that thing headed this way?" asked Mendoza.

"It is me," whispered Jenkins in a sheepish voice.

Everyone turned to see a small pool of blood running out from under Jenkins' cloak. Emrys said nothing; he only cupped his face in the palms of his hands as if to wipe away the anxiety. If the beast was charging because it smelled blood, human or otherwise, they had to assume that this was a hostile creature.

"...Holy shit, Jenkins..." Mendoza mumbled, but her voice had more pity than spite. With those words, everyone knew what had to be done.

"It is time to go hot," barked the Sergeant.

Everyone tossed their cloaks off and set their reticules on the beast who had now reached a full sprint. They opened fire but the first few rounds only seemed to chip away at its boney cranium.

"Back to the rover," Sergeant Clark yelled over the sounds of rapid bursts and bullet casings that danced on the hardened turf.

Emrys paused, only for a moment, and turned back to see that Jenkins was not moving. "Come on," he screamed passionately.

"I'll hold him off," Jenkins replied with a smirk on his face.

They both knew that he had no chance against the barreling beast. It was easily twice his weight and its muscles rippled with definition as it sprinted across the valley toward them. The slash across Jenkins' arm made it difficult for him to hold his rifle but he continued to do so, firing short bursts at the charging animal.

Emrys continued to run with the rest of the team and only turned back whenever he could. Reaching a peak along the trail, just before Jenkins was out of sight, Emrys turned for one last look. He watched as Jenkins continued to fire his weapon. His short bursts become a wild spray of fire as the sprinting beast drew closer and closer. It barely skipped a step as it clenched Jenkins between its snarling teeth and shook him like a play toy. In mere seconds he was dead and the beast tossed his ragged body against a thorny glass wall. The beast then turned and looked at Emrys before charging down the trail to meet them. Emrys wasted no more time in catching up to the rest of the team.

"Get in," screamed Mendoza.

Mendoza had already started the rover and had turned it around. Emrys jumped into the passenger seat just seconds before the beast rammed its boney crown into the side of the vehicle. His heart was bursting from his chest and he felt a kind of fear that he had never felt before. Watching Jenkins ripped to shreds made him realize how close to death he truly was, and how loudly it was knocking just outside his door.

Three loud knocks could be heard from the rear compartment. The Sergeant was ready to leave, and now. From a small sunroof panel, Emrys could see a turret mounted on the back of the rover. Once they were moving, Mendoza knocked once on the back compartment. Sergeant Clark opened the panel and mounted the turret. He began shooting furiously at the beast that was still relentlessly chasing them.

"Orbital Command, come in. Orbital Command, this is Lance Corporal Mendoza. We have been engaged by an extra terrestrial creature that is extremely hostile." Mendoza continued to repeat her message from the rovers' communication system until a response was heard.

"This is Orbital Command; we are waiting for you to return to the landing site. Slingshot will commence in T minus four minutes." The soothing voice of an operator could barely be heard over the deafening sounds of the turret fire behind them and the fiery hot casings that bounced on the rooftop.

Sliding on the slick terrain, the hardened ground made it difficult for the tires get traction. As each hit from the beast seemed to make the vehicle more unstable, the rover continued to fishtail from side to side. Emrys looked through the sunroof once again to check on the Sergeant, who was still lying on the trigger. Just then, the beast leaped onto the rover and snapped at the Sergeant's head but missed only because of his quick reflexes. Sergeant Clark attempted to turn the turret but the beast was too close, it was nearly on top of its barrel. Giving up on the turret, he pulled out his sidearm and aimed for the soft tissue inside of its snarling bite. He fired off several rounds which were enough to make the beast reel back and fall off of the rover.

The shifting weight from the falling beast was enough to make the rover lose control and topple over. Sliding on its side, the rover finally came to a stop after crashing into the remains of a small cluster of charred trees. Emrys and the others only had seconds to crawl out of the battered vehicle and check their weapons. Though it was out of sight, the loud whaling snorts from a distance were enough to let them know that the beast was still very much alive.

"Sarge, we have like three minutes. What do you want to do?" asked Mendoza.

A battered and beaten Sergeant Clark only looked at Mendoza but never said a word. Clark simply gave a subtle shake of his head as he pursed his lips. It was as if she instantly understood him; they were too far to reach the site in three minutes.

Barking out his final orders, the Sergeant pointed in the appropriate direction. "Emrys, I need you to head that way. The Slingshot is about four klicks. You just need to keep..."

"...Wait, four klicks? We have to get moving now," Emrys screamed. His heart was beating so fast that everything around him was a blur. He was hyper focused and yet nothing felt quite real; the rush of adrenaline seemed to take away his fears and replace them with a foggy resemblance of his surroundings. The only thought in his mind was reaching the Slingshot.

"Listen to me Warrant Officer," Sergeant Clark yelled at Emrys, tightly gripping his shoulder to get his attention. "Your job is to report what you saw here. Our job is to make sure that you get that chance." Clark once again gestured in the direction that Emrys needed to run.

As he sprinted down the path, Emrys could only hear a few faint orders from the Sergeant.

"...Mendoza, get on the Comm and tell OC to hold that Slingshot. We've got their Warrant Officer en route..."

Emrys raced down the lonely path where all he could hear was the sounds of his own breath, accented by the distant crackling of gunfire. The AR goggles were constantly reminding him of how far the marker was and how much longer it would take him at his approximated speed. He was frustrated by the accuracy of the timer that reminded him of the impossible task. Emrys continued to run until his lungs burned and his legs trembled, but he never lost a step.

As the timer in his goggles reached ten seconds, Emrys could see the marker was still two klicks away. His heart seemed to skip a beat for a moment and there was nothing else on his mind but reaching that marker. He sprinted harder and harder, hoping for more speed, visualizing his location just a few meters further followed by a few hundred meters then suddenly, it happened; he awakened.

Emrys could feel himself tearing apart cell by cell and forming into incandescent particles of light. It all happened so quickly and yet it felt like a lifetime for him to watch his body project itself to where he wished it to be. He sensed an ethereal image of himself materializing and his soul being absorbed into the new figure, but it was several hundred meters closer to the marker. Emrys tried again, then again and each leap was longer than the last. He appeared to be skipping through space almost instantly, reaching the marker with only a few seconds to spare.

Once inside of the Slingshot, Emrys buckled into his harness and waited for the last couple seconds to count down before being shot up into their air. The G forces were almost intolerable, but after what Emrys had just experienced he was happy to be alive. The sensation in his chest was amplified by the combination of extreme forces and the feeling of knowing that he escaped death by seconds, nearly the blink of an eye.

Rocketing through the atmospheric debris, Emrys could feel the Slingshot being pulled by Orbital Command's retractors. It only took a matter of seconds to reach from ground level on Seizonrenda to orbital distance. The Orbital Command vessel quickly picked up Emrys' free-floating dropship and settled it into the docking bay seamlessly. Still shivering from the adrenaline that coursed through his veins, he could feel his heart pressing against the harness that kept him steady. After all that he had seen, Emrys had only one wish; never to see Seizonrenda again.

Chapter 21

In the town center, Amara sat on the bench that she enjoyed so much. She looked over the town and its people and enjoyed the low rumbling sounds of a small town developing into something greater. Several new construction projects had begun near the outer ring of the town and she wondered what Emrys would think of them upon his return.

Though the atmosphere of the people on Harvest seemed unchanged, the world around them seemed to be growing faster than anyone had anticipated. Amara wondered if the recent explosion of resources being exported from the mines had something to do with the economic boom. It seemed like every shop and corner store was flourishing and new businesses were opening every day, but she found it strange that no one questioned where the wealth was coming from. Everyone simply treated the new found wealth of the town as a gift and continued with their lives, never questioning who the gift was from.

Witnessing the changing tides around her, Amara was no stranger to these occurrences. She had seen displaced colonies and tribes on Earth, slowly devoured by the black hole that is the UMI. The sheer size and influence of such a military power was absolute; any insurgency in UMI history has proven that. The inevitable event horizon had been reached on Serec, and Harvest was being dragged in like every other colony in past times.

The influences of the UMI were everywhere, and though Amara did not care one way or the other she could not help but feel remorse for the lifestyle that she first saw in Harvest. The low-tech town that first welcomed her there was becoming less a town and more like a UMI sanctioned colony. Along the center hub, where many of the older stores and bistros rested, Amara could see them renovating their exteriors to keep pace with the new construction. An almost inaudible sigh escaped her lips as she found herself missing the chaotic appearance of the more weathered structures throughout Harvest. One by one, the buildings were becoming newer and more illuminated renditions of themselves. Her thoughts were quickly interrupted by a familiar voice.

"Just the person I was hoping to see," said an elder woman. She was the same woman that Amara had met there before.

"Can I help you with something?" Amara asked in a polite tone, returning a trained smile.

Just as she had done before, Amara watched as the elder woman sat down next to her. Amara shuffled slight to the side to give the elder woman some breathing room on the bench that was built for two. Waiting patiently for a response, Amara found it strange that the woman was intent to find her. They had only met once before after all, hardly enough time for such kind words.

Amara speculated that the woman had no one else, no family or friends. It was not a Mencist analysis but more of an instinctual reaction. She imagined herself doing the same if she had lived a lifetime without meeting someone like Emrys, without having someone to share their thoughts with. Perhaps these fleeting moments with strangers was all that one could hope for when they did not have a friend at their side.

"Oh, I was merely hoping for some company on my last bath in the Serec sun," replied the elder woman. Her tone was mournful and she appeared more agitated than Amara recalled.

The elder woman held a small walking stick, an accessory that Amara did not recall from their last visit. She watched the woman hold the stick on her far side and simply tap it on the ground every few seconds as if to break the silence. Amara questioned if the woman had the stick to help her move around. She appeared to be strong enough not to need it, but Amara assumed that her health must have degraded since they last met.

"Are you going somewhere?" Amara asked, wondering why she would suddenly choose to leave the planet. It certainly appeared that she loved her time on Serec and yet she sounded eager to leave.

"I am afraid that this is my last day on Serec. Some of my greatest achievements were right here in Harvest. It truly will be a shame to let it all go," the elder woman nearly mumbled her words. She was almost too busy admiring the sun to give a meaningful response to Amara. "Tell me, if you knew exactly how long you had to live, what would you do with your time?" the woman asked in a solemn voice.

"Are you dying?" Amara inquired. The words came from her mouth so quickly that she barely stopped to think if they were appropriate. Still, she did want to know, and it appeared that her time with the elder woman was passing quickly.

"Oh Heavens, I hope not. It is hard to say." The woman chuckled, followed by a raspy cough. "As the Chief Professor in the Medical Research Advisory to the UMI Council, we can be subject to the most experimental of procedures. I assure you that the long title merely earns me a rank that is above most commissioned officers but rarely grants me the freedom that one might expect." The professor seemed tired and worn, and her once acute sensory seemed slightly more dull than Amara recalled.

"Did you ever plant those seeds?" The professor asked with a curious tone.

"No... I am afraid that I don't share the same faith in the unknown as you. Keeping them around my neck is a known quantity that I am willing to live with. It is how I choose to remember Earth." Puzzled by the question, Amara looked at the woman to determine if she was being genuine. The professor's once acute awareness seemed to be fading. Amara wondered what had changed since their last brief reunion.

"I see there is no convincing you, but I suppose it is to be expected of a Mencist" the professor said with sigh.

Caught off guard, Amara straighten up slightly and looked to the professor once again. She did not recall mentioning anything about being a Mencist. This woman had clearly mediated with several Mencist in her time to have made that conclusion so quickly. Having shared only surface deep ambitions with this woman, Amara was suddenly reminded that she was in the presence of a high level UMI official.

"I really should be leaving now, Amara... I never did get your full name."

"Binson. My name is Amara Binson."

"How interesting," the woman grunted as she stood to her feet.

Amara could now more easily see that the professor was less stable on her feet. Feeling around her general area with her walking stick, the woman practically stumbled over nearby debris. It was something that she might have once noticed long before it was under her feet. The woman tapped the stick on the ground, pausing to absorb the echoes before appearing more surefooted with her following steps.

"The UMI insignia," Amara noted. It was enough to give the woman pause.

Amara was referring to the patch on the woman's white uniform. It was the distinctive broken hilt of a legendary sword, cradled by the U shaped arch of the union, and anchored with iron wings that looked like godly rays of light. It was a sign that is difficult to misinterpret, a menacing and powerful message that displayed the pillars of the UMI philosophies. The professor gave a subtle scowl before she promptly covered it with her scarf.

"Do you know of my father, Miles Binson? He was supposed to return over a week ago." Amara waited but the woman only stood there and stared for a moment.

In time, a polite smile painted the woman's face, "You will be seeing him soon, I am certain of it."

"Thank you," Amara replied, returning a trained smile. A trained smile was the least that she could do since Amara could only assume that the elder woman, the professor, was nearing the end of her own life.

Long after the professor stepped away, Amara decided to leave her place on the lonely bench as well. She still had her concerns over the late return of the fleet vessel and wondered why Emrys had not sent any further audio logs. The radio silence was beginning fray her usual cool and apathetic composure. She wondered if Emrys' father had more news of his son, though the brief passing that she had in the mines did not paint the strongest of family ties.

Drifting through the serpentine paths that control the flow of pedestrians as much as it did the sand and wind, Amara made her way to the tram station. It was still midday and she reckoned that his father would still be working at the dig site. She did not know much about the man but she gathered enough information to reason that he was a diligent worker and someone who had invested his life into Harvest. At this time in the day, there was no other place that he could be.

The ride on the tram was swift but Amara could feel the beginnings of wear in the magnetic levitation. The occasional bump along the trail showed signs of weakened joints along track though it was hardly enough to be concerned with. She knew that the tram had gotten an excessive amount of use in the recent weeks. Since their deposit findings several weeks ago, it seems that the tram had been used for everything from staff to cargo. It was only a matter of time before repairs would become a part of the routine, though she did wonder who would be responsible for the expensive repairs; the Harvest miners or the UMI Civilian Assistance program. In her heart, she knew the answer to that. Taxing the working force was how the UMI maintained a pulse on the economy and repairs for transportation were no different.

Amara stepped up to the rickety door of Cole's trailer, his office that sat just outside of the cave entrance. She gave a subtle knock at first but no one answered and so she knocked louder. After a brief minute, a man stepped up to the door and nudged it open slowly.

"You wouldn't know this, but there is no private place on this site," said Cole. "You can knock, but we open our own doors around here."

Cole's groggily voice told Amara that he must have been sneaking a few brief moments of sleep. He looked worse for wear and smelled like he had not showered in a few days. The toll of his success was clearly showing on his weary face and solemn tone, and the condition of his office told her that he must have been using it as both an office and sleeping quarters.

"I am sorry to intrude," Amara said in a formal manner. She waited briefly for Cole to respond but he only gestured lazily for her to continue. "You are Emrys' father correct?"

A raspy chuckle erupted from the seemingly elder man. He let his fatigued body carry him back to his office chair

and sank into it with a heavy sigh. Rubbing away the
crusted signs of tired and dusty eyes from his face, Cole
leaned back to one side and stared at Amara from head to
toe. He inspected her jumpsuit that was no doubt made
with the finest threads, and lingered on the scarf-like
cloth that gently molded over her shoulders and down
around her arms. Her elegant erect posture was a sure
sign of etiquette training and left Cole with a puzzled
look on his face. It was as if he questioned why a
beautiful young woman from class A would be searching
for Emrys, a miners' son.

"And who might be asking?" demanded Cole. A
puzzled looked still colored his chalky face.

"My name is Amara and Emrys is my..." Amara
stopped and gave her words careful thought. The UMI
was not popular amongst the miners; she gathered that
much from Emrys, and her last name would surely say
more than she wanted to reveal at the time. "He is my
friend," she said in a stuttering voice.

The words were difficult to come by but they were
true. Still, using herself in the context of having a friend
had a ring to it that sounded unreal, like it was a lie. But
Mencists are rarely capable of lying unless it made tactical
sense and she had no reason to lie. It must have been
true. She rationalized her friend in her mind as she had
done so many times before and it warmed her heart.

"You are a strange one," Cole mumbled, "I am starting
to see why you two are friends." He chuckled again in his
raspy voice, this time his tone was friendlier than before.

"I wanted to ask if you have heard from Emrys,"
Amara posed the question in the most polite way that she
could. She understood that it was a delicate matter and
did not want to raise any concern.

"No... No I haven't. The last thing I got from him was
a note in my inbox. He said he was going on a mission

but didn't say where he was going or how long he would be gone," replied Cole.

"That is fairly standard protocol. Security measures are very strict for low profile missions," Amara was not sure if her words were of any comfort to Cole but it was all she had to offer him.

Cole did not reply immediately, he only sat in his sunken chair and stared through Amara. It appeared as if he was not in the room and Amara began to shift from side to side, hoping that it might awaken Cole from his dazed appearance if he saw movement in his sights. Her efforts were in vein and Cole continued to look off and occasionally show a crooked smile as if he had been reminiscing of a time long ago.

"We used to have it out," chuckled Cole. Amara found it strange that Cole would laugh over a violent altercation but it obviously seemed like their way of communicating, their twisted way of showing that they cared for each other. "He was a fighter, that kid. He used to come home every day, bruised up from some fight. I don't wager that he won much," Cole let out a laugh that sounded like he half wanted to cry. It was as if the mere thought of his son was pulling at his heartstrings, playing with his emotions. Amara could see that Cole missed his son, words that he would never say to Emrys.

"He never was very coordinated," offered Amara.

Thinking back to her first impressions, she envisioned that clumsy young man who was tripping and panting as he ran up to greet her upon her arrival to Serec. Amara felt confident that it was an image that seemed fairly consistent for him.

"So you do know him well," Cole replied with a smile on his face. "I remember, he came home one day from the academy – this was when we were still on Earth – he was cut and bruised up real good. His arm was all cut up, but he wouldn't say why; pride I guess. Meyra wasn't too

amused at the time, she never was. She was a better
mother than I ever was as a father, I'll tell you that
much."

"I know he cares about you," Amara commented,
though it was only a half truth.

Amara recalled that Emrys had mentioned Cole and
never actually said anything nice about him, but from the
tone that Emrys used when he spoke about his father, she
could extract that there was an emotional connection
between them. It certainly was not a perfect relationship,
but she could see that they held some level of affection
and respect for one another. The connection was easier to
read in Cole's misty pink eyes than in Emrys.

"I've been a fool. I only kept this site running for this
long because I wanted to keep the family together. I
wanted to keep Meyra alive just a little while longer. This
dig site... It was just as much a part of her as it was for
me and I couldn't let it go."

"Is that why you let him enlist?" Amara asked.

"He is a grown man and I can't bind him by the
shackles of my own life. It is a father's dream to someday
be succeeded by his children. I suppose enlisting was his
way of doing that; pride I guess." Cole chuckled again at
his repetitiveness. Pride seemed to be a theme
surrounding Emrys.

"Pride?" asked Amara. She found it odd that Cole
would use pride as freely as an excuse for all of Emrys'
actions. His fighting spirit, his eagerness to achieve
greatness, and even his bullish efforts to gain her
friendship; they were all attributed to his pride?

"...funny thing about pride is that it doesn't have to be
a feeling. Pride can be a place, a trinket, a memory..."
Cole paused briefly, noticing that Amara had clutched the
locket around her neck. She was entranced by his fast and
loose description of a word that once seemed to only have
a textbook definition before now.

Cole stared squarely at the young woman standing in front of him before saying, "Pride can even be a person that you wish to protect."

A bit lost by his final words, Amara did not understand what he meant when he said that pride could be a person. While trying to decipher the meaning of his words, Amara looked down at her watch and her eyes widened. The day had passed more quickly than she had anticipated. She still had much to do to prepare for the return of her father and her friend, whenever that may be.

"I really must be going," Amara said in a polite voice. "Thank you for your time."

Cole merely nudged his head slightly to the side, giving her a tired but welcoming nod. "Anytime, Amara..." he hung on her name as if he was asking for her full title.

"Thank you again," she replied as she darted out of the rickety doorway.

Amara found it strange that Emrys' father used the same inviting words as Emrys himself often did. *Anytime, Amara* - Those words rang in her ear like a distant dream, one that she simply could not remember.

Chapter 22

Standing in front of a large glass display that stretched at least 2 meters wide and just as tall, Emrys was awaited patiently. The brushed metal walls of the control room were littered with dials and digital screens, and the people working at each station diligently maintained the ships systems. Listening to the beeps and buzzes of the tactile feedback devices was annoying at first, but in time they slowly faded into the ambient noise of the ship. Having recovered from his hair-raising experience, Emrys could not help but be anxious to complete the debriefing and hopefully close the door on his first mission. It was not long before the screen became active and professor was staring down at Emrys who promptly saluted.

"Let us skip the pleasantries Warrant Officer and get to the facts," the professor stated firmly. Emrys could see the professor swiping her finger up and down her tablet and mouthing the words that she was reading. "I have finished your report but I must say that it is all very hard to believe."

"The events occurred as the report describes," Emrys explained in a steady tone, "We attempted to make contact with the rest of my team for a period of 7 days but received no response."

"Similar reports were being made across the map which is why it has taken us this long to report back," Colonel Miles interrupted, "We've been busy picking up our men around the globe, whoever was left that is."

"Professor, what we saw down there was..." Emrys tried to justify the words in his report but was quickly shut down.

"Don't get ahead of yourself, WO Hughend. My first responsibility is you," explained the professor. She ignored the curious look on Emrys' face and continued to sift through the digital documents. "Are you trying to tell me that you," she paused again to find the word in her report, "blinked? Is that the word that you would use to describe your awakening?" she asked in a doubtful voice.

"It is the best word that I could find, professor," Emrys replied, again in his unwavering tone. "I can't explain it but..."

"...then by all means let me," she replied. Her voice was slightly elevated and her tone was bordering on hostile which told Emrys that she had her doubts. "In order to achieve a temporal warp you would need to accelerate the particles in your body such that they reach a quantum state. In order to do that, without spontaneously combusting in an oxygen filled environment, it would require that you biologically produce an ion field that is able to repel the matter around you; an anti-matter bubble. Can you do that WO Hughend?"

"I am not a scientist and frankly I do not even know or understand the chemicals that you have injected into my body. All I know is that I traveled over two kilometers in less than five seconds, over the course of four maybe five short jumps." Each word from Emrys was growing in volume but he quickly calmed himself down. Now would not be the time to worsen her opinion of him.

"...and then it seems that you passed out from the exhaustion of using your newly found ability. Interesting," the professor mumbled to herself as she typed feverishly to amend her own notes to the report.

"How long exactly did you sleep after pushing yourself so hard?"

"The medical tech explained that I fell asleep in my quarters but did not wake up for nearly 24 hours. I awoke in the sick bay," Emrys replied. "I admit that my jumps were rough and they expelled a lot of my strength, but I do feel like I have a better understanding now."

From her brow-raised response to his comment, she had a clear interest in Emrys and he was not quite sure how to feel about that, not yet. After his latest encounters with the professor, the last thing on his mind was spending more time with her. An illuminated grin was painted across the professor's face; she looked almost proud to hear those words from his lips. It was the kind of jubilation that one would expect from a scientist who may have witnessed the birth of a new kind of human, a new kind of soldier. It was hard to know exactly why a descendent of the rebellion would be so proud to offer a higher class of soldier to the UMI, but as Emrys was told before, she had her reasons. It was wiser to leave the professor alone, and prodding for those answers now would have been a futile endeavor.

"Professor, about my report," Emrys tried to bring the conversation back on track. It was apparent that the professor was more concerned about him but there was a larger threat at hand. "From the data that I have gathered it is clear to me that we are dealing with a highly intelligent race."

"...go on," the professor begrudgingly pressed for Emrys to continue. The frustrated sigh that followed said that she wanted to keep on Emrys, but she understood that her own scientific interests could not consume the debriefing.

"The master species, the one who controlled the beast; he seemed to have an innate connection with the creature.

It was as if he spoke to it in a language that they both understood."

"You keep saying, He. Are you proposing that this creature is somehow human," she asked.

"Well, no. He... She... It," Emrys finally settled on the non-descript word before he continued after a long and anxious sigh, "It was human-like, a walking biped with opposable thumbs but it looked much more powerful. Also, the beast that killed Pvt. Jenkins never skipped a step before tearing him in half. If arthropodology has taught us anything, it is that their frame and form are designed for light weight, incredible strength, and resilience."

"...and from your report, you claim that there is enough evidence to suggest that the artifact near Harvest is in fact a ship belonging to this alien species; this bug species," the professors words were mocking and barely audible over her own snickering.

"Not only is that the case, but the production of Dust is somehow connected to this species. This could very well have been the catalyst for all of our technological advancements in the last millennium, maybe longer. This is an intelligent species, professor." Emrys continued to drive his last point over and over, stressing each word. It all seemed to fall on deaf ears as he tried to explain the severity of the situation, the gap of intelligence between humankind and this new species.

"We are requesting immediate backup from the remainder of the fleet in Serec to..." Miles attempted to expedite the debriefing but was promptly interrupted.

"Colonel Miles Binson, there is no remaining fleet," the professor replied to an audience of gasping voices from the command crew within the ship, Miles included.

"The fleet was en route from Earth and scheduled to arrive a week ago. What happen?" Miles barked his words like an angry dog and Emrys watched the Colonel's fists ball up as they squeezed the edge of the table that suspended the massive screen.

"The fleet arrived right on schedule, but I regret to inform you that all UMI soldiers are being evacuated. The Council has ruled from the initial reports that a quarantine of the insect threat is required. It shames me that such a brilliant specimen like you Emrys will be out of my reach."

Miles continued to press the professor, who was barely listening as she fiddled with her tablet. "This is not quarantine, it is a retreat; we both know that. We need assistance now; our ship is a scouting vessel not a battle cruiser. If the reports are correct then we have reason to believe that they are a highly militarized species and likely capable of intergalactic space travel." He was becoming more enraged with each exchange and was nearly screaming by the time he had said his last words. "These creatures *will* reach Serec, and in time they *will* reach Earth."

"Oh it is no doubt that they will reach Serec. The alien ship in Harvest is one of their own after all." The professors' words were candid and said with a half smile.

"That is it; isn't it?" Emrys speculated, confirming his suspicions out loud. It was as if a light had turn on in his mind. "This has nothing to do with minimizing casualties or tactical quarantines." Emrys turned to Miles who was too angry to connect the dots, and the puzzled look on his face begged Emrys to continue. Emry turned back to the screen before he explained, "This has everything to do with your damn religion."

"Preposterous claim of hostile seven foot insects being the true source of our Omniscient Rector is frankly unacceptable for the UMI. This is exactly the kind of rumors that the UMI must unfortunately exterminate at the source and sooner is always better than later," she explained in a calm and rhythmic voice. "Faith in the

Rector is more than a religion now; it is the economic foundation of Earth and the UMI. Did you really think that they would allow you to shake their foundation with outrageous assertions like those?"

"Professor now is not the time for your bible studies. We have hundreds of men and women on this ship, good soldiers on... this... ship... And we have hundreds of thousands of settlers on Serec..." Miles barked out and was once again interrupted.

"...and we have tens of billions of human lives on Earth. What is your point Colonel? Because if you are trying to play the numbers game with me, I assure you that Earth will always win." The professor began to raise her voice but was soon quieted by a coughing fit.

After clearing her throat one last time the professor sat up straight and matted down the wrinkles in her uniform. "Colonel Miles Binson and the crew of the fleet vessel Taharka, I'd like to take this time to thank you for your years of service. This is likely my final message for you and the loved ones that you leave on Serec. God speed everyone; may the Omniscient Rector of the cosmos shine his grace on you all."

Static was the only sound that followed her last words; even the crew remained silent, waiting for the Colonel to issue his next command. The professor had just sentenced them all to death for a lifetime of loyal service. Emrys could see the face of a defeated man standing in front of him, a man who had devoted himself to the UMI and would now be erased from history. The mixed emotions on his face told a complex story that Emrys could not hope to piece together, and the only clear emotion to shine through was shock and disbelief.

In that moment the Taharka was rocked by a hail of weapon fire as alien ships began to appear on the motions sensors. It was unclear if they had some form of warp device or were cloaked and following the Taharka from the beginning. They may have been there, watching them the entire time and monitoring them from the moment that they had approached Seizorrenda. The thought of them prowling the ship gave Emrys chills down his spine, and he instead focused on the most urgent concern of staying alive.

"Your orders Colonel," yelled Emrys. Miles meandered on his decision for some time and the crew waited silently for his command. "Your orders Colonel," Emrys screamed one last time. It was enough to jolt Miles from his stupor.

"Abandon ship. Use every escape pod and dropship we have to get back to Harvest," shouted Miles.

"What if the Evac ships have already left," a crewman asked.

"...then you'll have a better chance of hiding on the surface than floating around in the dead of space. This ship is going to be full of plasma induced holes in about two minutes, so I would suggest that you make your departures quick." Miles stood firm and his words were assertive but Emrys could see the fear in his eyes. He was afraid of something, but it wasn't death.

"Emrys," Miles called out.

"Sir!" Emrys exclaimed.

"Take the Captains pod; it's the fastest one on this ship." Miles ignored the puzzled look on Emrys' face and continued to explain, "Make sure that Amara lives through this. This is not an order Warrant Officer, this is me begging you. Will you do it for me?"

"Even if you didn't ask... Colonel," Emrys replied. "How will you get back to Harvest?"

"I need to make sure that everyone gets off of this ship. That is my priority; yours is Amara, now go," Miles hollered. His voice was barely audible over the sounds of twisting metal and shattered oxygen lines.

Emrys took the launch codes from Miles and darted down the corridor. Pushing against the flow of bodies that crammed the halls, he dodged between the passing crew members who were scrambling to reach the pods in time. A few familiar faces grazed by his peripheral view, but he had little time to worry about everyone on the ship; his objective was waiting on Serec.

Heading for the Captains pod, Emrys was lucky enough to be running away from the congested halls that lead to the launch bays. Reaching the pod with relatively little effort, Emrys punched the codes in feverishly and, in his haste, nearly forgot to harness himself before slamming his fist onto the launch button. In a flash, Emrys was on a jet set course for a Harvest landing in T minus 4 hours. Using this moment of solitude, Emrys did everything he could to revise his plans to save Amara and anyone else along the way. There would no time for strategy once he landed, and he knew that instinct would have to take over. Four hours was not a lot of time to develop a strategy, but for someone as prepared as Emrys, that time would be an eternity.

Chapter 23

Another week had passed since Amara had spoken with Cole. The long days of patiently waiting for their return had slowly degraded into a sickness inducing worry. She had grown tired of pacing through the empty house, a place that was too large for any one person to enjoy alone. It made her almost long for the cramped spaces of her living quarter back on Earth.

Sitting in the modern but blandly decorated den, Amara briefly reminisced on the disheveled historic building on Earth and its arcane security systems that she used to mock. It was a place that she would have never thought to miss, but it was not the building that she missed, it was the people. At least when her father was away on tour she had the ambient clamor of crowded streets and noisy neighbors. Even the security guard, the person that Amara gave little more than the occasional glance, he was a reminder that she was not alone. Now, on Harvest, the silence was burrowing into her mind, making her feel sick and lonely.

Sequenced images, visions of her early reprogramming would flash in the corners of her mind as the long days of solitude began to surface memories of her tortured past. Her cool and collected demeanor was quickly breaking down, and Amara had few clues to explain the phenomenon. The once refreshing home slowly turned into a voluntary prison cell, and Amara spent her days convincing herself that Miles would be home any minute now. She had refused to leave her home even though she knew that something had to change, she would have to change. Though it had only been a few weeks past their scheduled arrival, the reality of living alone was beginning to set in. Amara knew better than anyone that the UMI was punctual when it came to military assignments, executing with surgical precision. Amara imagined herself living a life much like the elder woman that she had met several times before, seeking companionship through idle conversations.

Amara would have never imagined such a feeling. "Am I, depressed?" she mumbled to herself. Looking around the room, Amara half expected a response but none came her way. The thought of her talking and knowing that no one was there to listen only made her feel more awkward and alone. Her once spotless mind was changing, and the apathetic logic of a Mencist was being replaced with human fears of loneliness and desperation.

Looking through the large window in the den, Amara questioned if thinking like a normal human being was worth the trouble of carrying all of the grief and suffering that followed the brief heartwarming moments. Her greatest fears of losing everyone seemed all the more real and yet those fears only seemed to have manifested in the short seasons that she has lived in Harvest. Two weeks had passed with no communication from the fleet ship; two weeks, four days, sixteen hours, and twenty-seven minutes. The clock in her mind was as sharp and consistent as the incessant ticking of an early seventieth century pendulum clock. It was driving her mad and she needed to get outside.

The cold chill of the early winter season felt like pins and needles on Amara's face but she refused to stay inside any longer. Thankfully, it did not snow in Harvest. The tilt of the planet and the salted sands made it a hostile environment for any frost to survive the night, let alone the daylight. Despite the frostless terrain, the winters were still very cold and required more than a simple jumpsuit.

Amara covered her shoulders and arms with a fashionable scarf and coat that was well fitted past her hips and down her legs. She was slightly ashamed to be wearing the coat since it was meticulously crafted by a known designer, tailored and worth more than some people might make to survive in Harvest. The coat was only one of many she had just like it and a reminder of the life that she once lived on Earth. Amara did not miss the foul nature of the high society that she was once surround by, and she wondered if the culture in Harvest and the hard times they had lived were related. She was starting to see the connection of their humble nature and their humble beginnings on Serec. It made her question if the recent explosion of the economy would lead to the same distant separation of the people, as it did on Earth.

Though disappointed for not having bought winter apparel that was more appropriate for Harvest, Amara ventured out of the house in her coat. She told herself that she would purchase a new coat when they arrived, when Miles and Emrys returned. Amara was hopeful that Emrys would aid her in finding a wardrobe that helped her feel more like a native and less like the visitor who lived on the hilltop.

As she often did, Amara found her way back to the town center, but this time she did not choose to sit high up and away from the crowd. Amara found a bench that rested just outside of the hollow courtyard that marked the center of the town. It was one of the first places where she had started to learn more about Emrys and it sparked an image in her mind, the image that she had cataloged many seasons ago of a jittery and nervous young man who did not have enough to pay for his meal. Closing her eyes, Amara recalled the narration that she had tied to the imagery. Amara was amazed at how different one person could be in such a short time, the words that she extracted from her databanks barely sounded like her.

The words that Emrys spoke to her long ago were starting to make sense now, "Besides, you would be surprised at how quickly the mind heals." That was what he had said, and now she was beginning to see his point. She felt more alive in recent months than she ever did on Earth, and the suffering emotions were part of living. She still questioned if the mind of a normal human or a reprogrammed human was better, but Amara did enjoy the new person that she had become, even if it was painful at times.

The cabin fever was beginning to wear thin as positive thoughts surged through her. The imagery of Emrys and his clumsy appearance was complimented by the cool air and chaotic but subdued sounds of the town center. It was an experience that she would have never had if her father had not brought her to Harvest or if she had never met Emrys. She felt unique and special for having these serendipitous series of events lead her down this path in life.

With the image of Emrys so fresh in her mind, Amara held on to the shameful expression that she saw that day. In her hand was the tablet that she carried with her at most times. She opened the tablet and started a blank canvas which appeared with a number of digital paints and brushes. Amara continued to scribe the image in her mind onto the tablet, and for a short while she was gone to the world. That world had faded into the background of her consciousness, serving as the inspiration for the colors and strokes that filled the corners of her digital painting.

An advisory warning beacon stopped Amara in her tracks and her heart skipped a beat; her trance had been broken. The beacon that rang through the town was like a jolt of electricity that left her paralyzed and she immediately thought of her fears once again. With a sudden rush of blood rising to her head, Amara felt faint for a brief instance as her vision widened and she could now see the image that she had scribed in her trance. As the half finished portrait of Emrys stared back at her, she could not help but wonder what was about to be said.

"Warning, warning, warning," an operators voice could be heard on all channels.

The communication signal was being broadcasted across the data-link networks and any media device that responded. Amara's painting was overlaid by an audio message that continued to deliver information about the imminent threat.

"This is the UMI scouting fleet vessel, Taharka... We are broadcasting on all short wave burst frequencies... Our planetary entry systems are inoperable but the crew of the Taharka is being sent to Harvest by dropships." The operator spoke in a calm voice, as most A.I. operators did, but Amara was put off by the message.

If they were broadcasting on short wave frequencies then it must have meant that they were at least in the galaxy's inner limits. She was confused by why they would be sending soldiers down to the planet and not protecting the planet from orbital height. The message was conflicted and did not make tactical sense, unless the Taharka was badly damaged and they were fleeing to Serec. If this was the case, the message was likely intended to avoid a panic amongst the civilians. Amara continued to listen to the message, dissecting half-truths and analyzing each cryptic phrase as a Mencist would.

As the message continued, Amara stopped to look around at the people. The town center that was once a melting pot of UMI soldiers and civilians was now plastered with only civilians. The military population was gone, vanished without a trace. She wondered how long it had been this way. Amara pressed herself to remember but it was difficult; she had been locked in her home for over two weeks. The only exception may have been the day she went to speak to Emrys' father, but Amara pressed again to remember more.

The last UMI solder she saw was... It was the professor. Amara's eyes widened as the conversion that she had with the elder woman raced through her head. It is likely that they were evacuating the soldiers in anticipation of some sort of planetary attack. The mere thought that the UMI had a threat to fear so much that they would abandon the planet left Amara nearly in tears of desperation. She felt helpless and could only sit and listen to the broadcast, the double meaning behind every word that was being said.

"...expect to see dropships falling within a one kilometer radius of the city. Do not, I repeat, do not attempt to intercept these dropships." The message continued to report conflicting statements, one after another.

The statements left Amara thinking that the operator must have been damaged. Whatever was happening up there, it was dire and she could sense that much. Amara knew that they must have been desperate to be broadcasting military procedures on a global data-link.

It was not long before the ships started dropping one after the other. The events were slow at first, one ship here and another there, but they quickly ratcheted up to dozens then hundreds of ships that appeared like fiery stars in the daytime sky. Observing their trajectory, Amara was now certain that the operator had been damaged. The ships were too close to each other, and too many clusters appeared to be targeting the same drop zones. The poor clustering could only mean that most of their guidance systems were likely disabled and the ships were falling straight down.

As the ships started to come into view Amara could see that some of them were riddled with holes and freefalling. Many others looked to have non functioning thrusters and were caught in a tail spin as they fell down to the surface, crashing against other ships on their way down. Raining down in a hailstorm of metal shards, many of the ships looked to be on a direct course for Harvest.

In what felt like the blink of an eye, ships began to crash down, all around Amara. They were spearheading through buildings and falling from the sky like balls of hellfire. In shock, Amara barely noticed the massive shard of a ship shoot past her, missing her by only a meter or less. The heat from the flaming hunk of metal was the only catalyst that stoked her to move away long after it crashed against the building wall behind her. She wondered aimlessly through the town center, watching as more ships littered the ground around her and mobs of innocent people were crushed under their weight.

A hard push from a panicked civilian nearly knocked Amara to the ground, but it was also what she needed to break loose from the shock in her system. Turning to see the civilian who had pushed her aside, Amara watched as the man darted away, and in an instant he was gone; sideswiped by a dropship that slid by, killing both the civilian and the person inside in a horrific explosion. In the background of all the devastation that Amara was witnessing, the operator continued to give instructions in a calm and soothing tone. Faint commands could be heard; remain indoors, and not to panic.

In the midst of the broken message, Amara only managed to make out one phrase; DEFCON 1. It was likely never meant for civilian ears but the operator lacked any data-link filters and continued to broadcast its messages openly. The amount of chatter on the data-link made it hard for Amara to concentrate and she had to disable it. As always however, she kept her tablet with her just in case more information became available.

In the moments following the DEFCON 1 status, a rain of plasma shells followed the dropships that were still falling down from the sky. Watching as the alien artillery cut through the falling ships effortlessly, Amara witnessed the dropships exploding in mid descent, reaching the ground in pieces of molten metal and organic ash. The plasma fire soon turned from the falling ships and down onto the crowded streets below. A few short bursts of the plasma rounds landed nearby and Amara watched them splatter like some kind of coagulated napalm. Everything it touched turned to flames and even the sandy floor crackled and sputtered like oil and water on a hot pan.

Though it was only minutes that had passed, it felt like an eternity for Amara to regain her composure. She raced down the main streets, toward the place that she called home for so many seasons now. Amara did not know why, but she had no place else to run and the town was no longer safe. She could only assume that if her father or Emrys were alive that they would look for her there. Hoping that they were alive was the only thing that gave her legs the strength to continue running.

Chapter 24

From the confines of his falling ship, Emrys could hear nothing but screams and nonsensical chatter through the communication systems. The operator was jabbering on open frequencies and Emrys could hear a small chirp for each ship that was shot down or failed to make the landing. The chirps were sounding off like artillery fire in his ear but the chatter became less cluttered and disorganized with each voice that stopped.

Emrys was coming in hot, too hot to stabilize his landing thrusters and the ship began to topple to its side and turn uncontrollably. The guidance systems were flashing red across the board and most of the auto-flight controls seemed to have lost their link with the Taharka. Either Orbital Command was destroyed or the operator had been too damaged to manage a connection with his dropship, but either way he had to eject. Emrys reached for the manual ejection lever and pulled, but nothing happened.

The dropship was in too hard of a tail spin and would not allow Emrys to eject. While sheets of metal peeled away from the G forces that threatened to tear the ship open, he raced through his options with the little time he had left. He watched the altimeter intently as it dropped faster and faster, the whole while he continued to pull back violently on the ejection lever. With only seconds to spare, Emrys blinked from the dropship and appeared on the ground below, only a few meters away from the ship which was still falling above him. Dodging the falling remains of the battered ship, Emrys barely escaped the explosion of shrapnel.

From his position, Emrys could see the dig site but no one was there, not on the surface anyhow. He speculated that Cole would have sent everyone home after a warning beacon, but Emrys briefly questioned if there were devices that could detect the beacon. In addition to his doubts, Emrys was not sure if Cole would have recognized the caverns as a safe retreat from a planetary threat. Casting aside his doubts, he reminded himself that there were too many variables to consider, and there was no time to waste.

Emrys staggered to his feet but he quickly fell back down onto one knee. Holding his head with one hand, he rubbed his temple to help keep the migraine-like pain and dizziness away. Emrys knew that the tail spin coupled with the use of his ability proved to be too much.

"I have to conserve it," Emrys reminded himself. If everything was going to work as he planned, he would need to conserve his strength for the moment when he absolutely needed it.

In the distance, the tram was headed toward Emrys and making its way back to Harvest. A leisurely trip on the tram was not his idea of fast travel but it was faster than running and safer than using his ability. As the tram rolled by, Emrys sprinted to keep up and just barely grabbed onto the tail end. From there, Emrys opened the emergency door in the back and made his way inside where he sank into one of the seats. Listening to the subtle rhythmic thumping of the tram gliding over the rails, he did his best to enjoy the brief moment of quiet serenity. The silence inside of the tram was the calm before the storm, before the total chaos that had likely consumed the town of Harvest.

In minutes, Emrys leapt off the tram that had barely come to a complete stop in the Harvest station. Not knowing where anyone was, he decided to stop at his father's hut since it was on the way to Amara's house. They were the most logical places to find anyone in Harvest since it had no disaster relief buildings or bomb shelters. Harvest was a peaceful and quiet town and, until today, did not have a need for a place to hide.

Reaching Cole's hut in record time, Emrys stormed in through the half opened door to find a man under a pile of rubble and molten plasma. Emrys could not tell how long the charred remains had been there or if Cole even knew what was happening in his final moments. The smell of burning flesh and debris left Emrys weak in the knees but he continued to fight to maintain his composure. He paced back and forth in the room, not knowing what to do next or where to go. Emrys' careful plan was beginning to unravel and he didn't know if he wanted to scream in anger or cry for the death of his father. It was all too much for him, so he decided to leave his father's remains in their place.

There wasn't enough time to identify the body or give him a proper burial, maybe not enough time to save Amara or himself. Not knowing the answers to any of the questions that clouded his mind, Emrys pressed on. With his father dead, nothing was certain anymore.

Emrys made his way through the back streets and serpentine paths, knowing that the town center would be mobbed with civilians trying to reach the space port. The main road might have been a shorter path but it likely would have taken twice as long and those were precious seconds that he could not afford to give. Emrys raced down the back streets until he reached Amara's house which had been partly destroyed. Many pieces of the roof appeared to have collapsed and the walls were buckling and swaying in the wind.

Knocking through the door with his bare shoulder, Emrys was able to break into the weakened home. "Amara!" Emrys called out for her, repeatedly. He ran through every room that was still standing until he eventually found her. Upstairs, sitting quietly and staring out of her bedroom window, Amara hardly flinched by the door that was kicked in so hard that it nearly came off of its braces.

"I used to smell cloves that blew in through these windows. I wonder where they have gone." Amara was talking nonsense; she was severely shell shocked and barely acknowledged Emrys or the crumbling building around her. Finally Amara turned to Emrys, and with a lifeless voice she asked, "Miles... My father... He is dead; isn't he?"

The sounds of chaos outside almost faded away for Emrys and only the sound of his heart remained. He had not seen her in what felt like a lifetime even though it had only been months. The anxiety of being so close to her was overwhelming and was only made more intense by the devastation that surrounded them.

Emrys was shocked by her resolve, her acceptance that life was near its end. He simply nodded in response to her question as if it was the only thing he could do or say. He watched Amara calmly turn her attention back to the window as if she was waiting for someone else to arrive.

"Would you like to sit with me?" Amara asked in a calm and polite tone.

Emry could not believe what he heard. He could not believe that she had asked him to sit and wait for death with her, as if she knew that Death himself was on his way. With those shocking few words, Emrys returned to himself and the sounds of the world were once again at deafening levels. The sputtering of enemy ships that flew overhead reminded him that there wasn't much time left.

"Take this," Emrys insisted as he stuck a handful of pills in her mouth. "I know they are meant to be swallowed, and they taste terrible but you'll just have to chew them."

Reluctantly, Amara chewed the pills and the rancid flavor helped to break her trance. "What did you give me?" Each word from Amara was clear and deliberate which told Emrys that she was returning to herself.

"There's no time to explain." Emry grabbed her arm then wrested her down the stairs and away from the broken home.

Amara continued to be dragged away as she looked back and watched the last of her home collapse onto itself. The sputtering thrusters of the enemy ship were all that could be seen through the mist of embers that drifted up from the remains of her home. The dust swirled into tiny cyclones as it was absorbed through the ship's engines and out the other side. Amara continued to watch the suspended vessel hover around her home until she turned the corner, out of sight.

Racing to an unknown destination, Amara could feel her arm being pulled harder and harder. "You are hurting me!" She screamed forcefully for Emrys to let go, and finally he did.

"I'm sorry but we don't have much time," he yelled. His voice was barely audible over the screams of people and whistling of alien ships zipping over the building tops. Pulling Amara a little further, Emrys tucked under a bridge and waited for another ship to swing past them.

"You are going the wrong way; the evacuation ships must be waiting at the space port!" She screamed, trying to be heard over all of the noise.

"There are no evacuation ships! No one is coming to save us..." Emrys spoke faintly but his words still traveled to her ears, though they might as well have struck her through the heart.

His words seemed to linger in Amara's thoughts as she could do little more than hold him tighter to keep from falling. The news weakened her spirit but the urgency she felt from him gave her a glimmer of hope that they could survive, that there was a place to hide from Death.

It wasn't long before they reached the outskirts of the city, the place where they first connected. The alien pod was still resting just as she remembered it, sprawled on the ground, elevated only slightly by the debris formed from its original impact on this planet. Amara was glad to see the pod but was puzzled since it was only designed for entry; it had no mechanism to launch.

Emrys shuffled around the pod, searching for something that seemed to be hidden underneath the seasons of shifting sands. "Do you remember what I told you, what I said when we first came here?"

"That was a long time ago," Amara said to him in a defeated voice. A misty appearance began to form in the recesses of her eyes but she quickly dried them. "Why are you here? You are a UMI soldier. You had to have known about the evacuation... Why are you here?!" She continued to repeat her question, each time her intensity increased. Puzzled by his presences, Amara's voice seemed almost frustrated by his dimwitted choice to face death with her. She had accepted it and was ready, but now she wondered why Emrys was there, prolonging the inevitable or perhaps sharing her moment.

"Because I knew that you would be here." Emrys stated his words boldly, letting her know that he would not, he could not, survive until she was safe.

His bold, matter-of-fact statements were unfiltered, but Amara understood why. She knew that, when the world was coming to its final moments, there was little time for gentle words. Trying to swallow, Amara could feel a lump in her throat as she attempted to choke down the seriousness of his words.

Emrys pointed to the sky which looked like a celebration of lights behind the rolling clouds and gestured for her to look as well. Lowering his arm, he turned to meet Amara's eyes and say only a few last words of encouragement, "Most of those ships will not break orbit. The fleet has lost its grasp on the perimeter and these escape vessels have no defensive weaponry."

Amara was clearly not settled by his words and so he tried another approach. "Do you remember what I told you when we first came here?" he asked again. This time he grabbed her by both arms to force them to face each other. "Listen to me. The enemy has already started their assault. In a matter of minutes this planet will be nothing but glass and ash! I have seen it with my own eyes..."

"Look at this pod..." Amara exhaled with a defeated sigh. Pointing to the small pod that rested nearby, she shrugged her shoulders hopelessly. Unable to focus on his question, the thought of death looming over the horizon felt like a more pressing question at the time. "We barely fit together the first time. What makes you think that it's going to keep us safe now?"

Emrys motioned for her to step inside and she complied. There was little time to argue and simply proving her theory through actions would resolve their disagreement more quickly than talking about it.

"You see?" Amara said rightfully, "It was meant for maybe one person. I can barely fit in here myself."

Before she could say any more Emrys interrupted her. "...I know," he said with a smile. He quickly closed the pod door, sealing her inside. His carefully laid plan to save everyone had unraveled but he was determined to at least save Amara, if no one else. "I made a promise and where I am going, I can't take you..." Emrys said in a somber tone. His cryptic words were enough for Amara to assume the worst, considering the devastation that was just beyond the horizon.

Inside the pod, she could hear the air locks pressurizing and the bellowing sounds of the world outside fading to nothing. The silence was almost deafening to her, with only the unsteady rhythm of her own breath to let her know that her ears had not failed her. Looking through the glass-like display she could see him sitting on the pod, smiling. *That smile*, she thought. *Why do you always look at me with that same forced smile, like you pity me even when I had everything, you pity me. Even now, you smile.*

Amara could see the winds blowing harder outside, so hard that Emrys could barely keep his balance. He pointed at her, or rather through her, to a switch that rested just to her right side. It was a very familiar switch, the same one that she saw him toggle many seasons ago. Looking back to Emrys, he motioned for her to turn it on, so she did.

Listening to the message that followed, she remained fixated on her only friend who awaited death just inches away. The recording was clearly made many years before today. It was a bit unsettling to listen to the youthful voice in that message and look out to the man that he had become.

> *Amara, when I heard you were coming I was so excited. I have been working on this plan for a long time, but I probably won't see you for another decade. Space travel to Harvest does take a long time but I'll be here, waiting.*
>
> *If you are listening to this, it means that something terrible is happening. I know that you are probably furious with me right now; you always did have a temper. But I want you to know that I thought this through a long time ago, and it is the choice that I made*

*for both of us. I hope you can forgive me
someday, if that day ever comes.*

*I never did tell you why I smiled around
you so much at the academy. I guess... I
guess you make me happy but nothing ever
makes you happy, so I smile for the both of
us. Until you find something that makes you
smile, I will smile for the both of us.*

*I want you to smile but more importantly,
I want you to know that there is a wide world
of emotions out there other than apathy and
anger. I have been lucky enough to find it
here on Serec, and I want you to have that
chance too. There is joy and love and sadness
as well, and I want you to know them all
someday. I want you to know... Know that it
is okay to cry sometimes, or know that tears
don't always mean that you are sad.*

"You are such a damned fool! Why?" Amara screamed
but Emrys could not hear her and she knew.

Even as she beat her clenched fists on the glass-like
panel, it let out little more than a subtle thud. Still,
Amara kept beating on the panel until her hands were
numb and her breathing was deep and winded.
Eventually, she gave in to the fatigue and the pain. She
was ready to die and he took that from her and it did
infuriate her, just as Emrys speculated.

Amara could do nothing but sit and watch through
that clear panel as she listened to the closing words in the
recorded message. The sky grew brighter with each
passing moment and all she could do was sit and watch.
Feeling helpless she sensed the tears welling up again;
that human emotion was overtaking her again.

Is this fear, she thought. No; she knew that she was
safe, as safe as one could be from the approaching threat.

Feeling the aching pain in her chest, Amara came to the only logical conclusion. *Sadness*, she thought. Not apathy or anger but sadness was what came over her. Finally the tears became overwhelming, and Amara was just as confused as she was upset. She couldn't dry them away fast enough as they ran down her cheek and those tears did nothing to sooth the pain in her chest.

Forgetting to toggle the switch, Amara looked down briefly at the display that showed there was more to the recording. She thought that it was a mistake, the recording had been playing for some time but it was silent. As Amara reached to turn it off she heard two voices, faint at first but they grew louder over time. After listening for some time, she realized that it was her voice from the first time she had visited the pod.

Emrys must have recorded that fateful first day where they bonded on Serec. It was as if he knew that this time would come, or perhaps he just wanted to remember it always. Amara wondered how many times he must have come back to that pod to listen to that recording, and she knew that it was a question that she could never ask him. His life after all would be coming to an end while he was out there and she would be waiting inside, waiting for the threat to pass over, waiting in the silence that begged to drive her mad while she listened to voices from her past.

Outside, the sky was nearly a shade of blue and white that could only mean one thing; the invaders had begun flashing the planet. Emrys was right when he said that there would be nothing but ash and glass and that moment had arrived. Flakes of ash rained from the sky and began to cover the panel so much that he could barely see Amara inside. He gently wiped away a small window and mouthed the words, "goodbye, Amara" to her. Turning his head up to the sky with his eyes closed, he could feel the mounds of ash raining on his face. Through it all, he was still smiling. It was as if there was no other place in the galaxy that he'd rather be.

As Amara continued to listen to the old recording, she felt embarrassed about her rudeness to him. Looking out of the ash filled panel, she half-smiled at him; it was all she could offer in return for his gift of life to her. Through her blinding tears Amara could see him smiling back. Living a short time on Harvest, it helped her better understand Emrys now, more than she did upon her arrival to Serec. It helped her to understand the boy in that recording and what Cole meant when he said that Emrys had pride. But there was more to this recording than she recalled from that night. There was so much that she never paid attention to that day, not him or his words or his intentions.

> *"Why are you being so nice to me?"* - Amara
> *"Isn't it obvious?"* - Emrys

In that moment she discovered so many things, pieces of her past and memories that were hidden deep in her mind. She remembered a young boy who always stood for her at the academy, a boy who said nothing but the kindest words. He watched her and protected her, and like a guardian angel, he saved her from more than one dangerous and painful whipping. She was a foolish child, and he was the reason why she endured it all this time.

"He loved me. All this time, he loved me..." Amara was shocked to have been so blind. She beat on the panel furiously, her tears still flowing, screaming his name. Emrys eventually turned his attention away from the bright sky down to her. Amara finally mouthed the words, "I love you."

"I know," Emrys replied with a wink and a smile.

A flash of hot white light grazed over her view and the ground trembled in a way that she had never known. Even through the protected panel, Amara could feel the radiant heat from outside. It was too late to say anymore. Whatever Amara wanted to tell him, it was too late. Like a brief fleeting moment in time, Emrys was gone.

All that Amara could see now was an endless sprawl of ash that was spread across the planes. Distorted waves of heat rose from the concoction of decomposing grains of sand and tinder, and the once small islands of exotic vegetation were nothing more than a bubbling coil of char. For as far as Amara could see and imagine nothing was spared; neither a tree nor bush or human life survived, except one.

"No!" She let out blood curdling scream.

Amara beat her fist on the panel once more out of frustration. Sobbing and gasping for air, the pod suddenly felt so small and suffocating. She felt the weight of the world that had fallen on her, and all she could do was try to catch her breath between the lapses of panicked tears.

"I need to find him!" Amara screamed deliriously. "I need to know if he's okay!" She knew that what she was saying made no sense, but she had to know, she had to try. He might have lived somehow; he had to have survived...

In that moment, the pod's display began to scroll with red codes, most of them she could not understand. In her fatigued condition, Amara struggled to remember her academy research, her studies of the alien artifacts that were intertwined within the scriptures. She did her best to translate what she could from the rapid stream of codes and signals, the alien language. Scattered between the streams of codes were words, phrases that she could decipher.

External temperature above normal...
Carbon monoxide levels dangerous...
Plasma fallout levels potentially fatal...
Engaging cryogenics...

"Emrys!" Amara called for him over and over but she knew it was futile. She could feel the pod getting colder with each passing moment. She remembered the pills that Emrys had given her and a brief painful smile brushed across her face. He had planned every detail down to the sleep pack, the same pill pack that she took on her first cryogenic trip to Harvest.

It must be his pride I guess, she thought, reminiscing on Cole's words. In her final waking moments, Amara could see a ghost of Emrys, an ethereal specter in the peripheral of her eyes, watching over her. But she when turned to focus on him, the specter was gone. She wondered if it was his spirit or the delusions of her medication and the extreme cold that now filled the pod.

"Thank you, for everything," she said, looking out of the panel that was nearly concealed by a growing layer of soot and ash. She thanked Emrys for all that he had done. She wanted to thank him personally but never had the chance, not when he was alive and with her. Amara shed a joyful tear, knowing that all he would say was, "Anytime, Amara."

Amara's tears that once flowed freely down her cheeks were frozen in place and, in less than a blink, she was frozen in time.

About the Author

Benjamin Quintero is an indie videogame developer
and author, living in Raleigh, North Carolina. As a fan of
fictional storytelling and videogames, Benjamin has
turned his passions into a blossoming career that blends
the best of both worlds.